A. Night
in Beverly Hills

Also by Andrew J. Fenady
in Large Print:

Claws of the Eagle
Double Eagles
The Rebel: Johnny Yuma

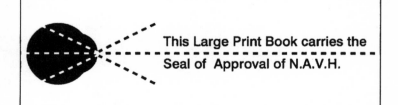

A. Night
in Beverly Hills

Andrew J. Fenady

Thorndike Press • Waterville, Maine

This novel is a work of fiction. Names, characters, places and incidents are either the product of the author's imagination, or, if real, used fictitiously.

Published in 2005 by arrangement with Tekno Books and Ed Gorman.

Thorndike Press® Large Print Mystery.

The tree indicium is a trademark of Thorndike Press.

The text of this Large Print edition is unabridged. Other aspects of the book may vary from the original edition.

Set in 16 pt. Plantin by Al Chase.

Printed in the United States on permanent paper.

Library of Congress Cataloging-in-Publication Data

Fenady, Andrew J.
  A. Night in Beverly Hills / by Andrew J. Fenady.
     p. cm. — (Thorndike Press large print mystery)
  ISBN 0-7862-7770-X (lg. print : hc : alk. paper)
  1. Private investigators — California — Los Angeles — Fiction. 2. Detective and mystery stories — Authorship — Fiction. 3. Beverly Hills (Calif.) — Fiction. 4. Jewel thieves — Fiction. 5. Large type books. I. Title. II. Thorndike Press large print mystery series.
  PS3556.E477N54 2005
  813'.54—dc22   2005008989

For Dorothy and
Robert Mitchum

And for Mary Frances

As the Founder/CEO of NAVH, the only national health agency solely devoted to those who, although not totally blind, have an eye disease which could lead to serious visual impairment, I am pleased to recognize Thorndike Press* as one of the leading publishers in the large print field.

Founded in 1954 in San Francisco to prepare large print textbooks for partially seeing children, NAVH became the pioneer and standard setting agency in the preparation of large type.

Today, those publishers who meet our standards carry the prestigious "Seal of Approval" indicating high quality large print. We are delighted that Thorndike Press is one of the publishers whose titles meet these standards. We are also pleased to recognize the significant contribution Thorndike Press is making in this important and growing field.

Lorraine H. Marchi, L.H.D.
Founder/CEO
NAVH

* Thorndike Press encompasses the following imprints: Thorndike, Wheeler, Walker and Large Print Press.

Chapter One

In that movie *Double Indemnity* Fred MacMurray staggered — bleeding and dying — to a Dictaphone machine to tell a story, to get the facts on the record. I am not bleeding at the moment, nor is death imminent as far as I know, but there is a story I've got to get on the record even though it's a story that can never be published, at least not in the foreseeable future.

I suppose I could go through all that rigmarole of changing names, dates and places and slapping on the usual disclaimer about the events being fictional, and any similarity to actual persons being coincidental, but then, what would be the point?

This way, I'll set down what really happened, even though I have to guess at some of the patches that made up the crazy quilt. But it all added up to a shroud — make that shrouds — for those people who are done with the business of breathing.

I'll let you know which things I'm guessing at, but then you'll be able to tell that anyhow, because I don't appear in those parts of the patchwork.

In those days my office was on the corner of Larchmont and Beverly in Hollywood. The sign on the frosted door read:

> # A. NIGHT
> ## Private Investigator

From the corner window near the roll-top desk I could see Paramount Studios and above that was the Griffith Observatory where they shot those scenes from *Rebel Without a Cause* with James Dean, Natalie Wood and Sal Mineo. In the movie that's where Sal Mineo died. In real life he died, too young, in an alley in Hollywood. All three died too young — Mineo, Dean and Natalie Wood.

For the last couple of years I could no longer see Paramount or the Observatory because some jerk had built a three-story building that effectively obscured my view.

But when this story starts I wasn't looking out of the office window. I was looking out of the window of a limousine, and I was dressed as a chauffeur — except most chauffeurs don't have .38 Police Specials tucked next to their hearts.

It started out strictly routine. Same as last

year — and the year before. Mrs. Cynthia Alderdyce had hired me to drive her and a couple pounds of rocks to and from Walter Annenberg's annual New Year's Eve party in Palm Desert. But this year things didn't turn out the same — not for her — for me — or for a few other people.

Out of what used to be sand and rock, the domain of snake and tortoise, Walter Annenberg, like Kubla Kahn, did a stately pleasure-dome decree enfolding sunny spots of greenery. But at that moment the spots of greenery were enfolded not by the sun. They were lit by moonlight and by hundreds of electrical globes and spotlights that illuminated ten million dollars' worth of real estate evacuated by the snakes and tortoises and currently populated by smiling citizens, some of whom had certain snake-like characteristics.

But not Cynthia Alderdyce. I liked the old girl. She was a spicy tomato. Up from the chorus line of the Copacabana to the gilded gardens of Beverly Hills and Palm Springs.

I sat behind the wheel of the Lincoln parked in the driveway, which was about the size of a baseball infield.

The Lincoln rested alongside a battalion of other limousines and expensive automobiles stationed at a discreet distance from the huge ornate double doors of the main house. A squad of attendants stood by the entrance flanked by a platoon of security guards.

From inside the mansion strains of "Auld Lang Syne" chopped through the night air — sometimes louder as a door opened, then closed, while some attendant attended to business. I had just dipped into my second daily deck of Lucky Strikes and let the fumes do their damnedest to damage my innards. I had promised my mother to give up smoking someday. But I never said which day, and besides my mother was nowhere in sight.

I pulled out my grandfather's gold pocket watch. It was a hunting case Elgin. Inside there was an inscription:

Alexander Nyktas

That was his name. It was mine too — except mine had been Anglicized to Alex Night by my father. I never questioned his decision — on that or very little else — but that's another story — and this was another year according to the Elgin — 12:01 a.m.

One of the double doors opened again and Cynthia Alderdyce appeared, sixty-something, still svelte, blue gown with

10

matching purse, classic coiffure — with throat and right wrist weighted with dazzling jeweled necklace and bracelet. She was escorted by Colin, her son of forty years. Colin was tall, tanned, tuxedoed and still in shape. Colin worked at staying in shape. That's about all he worked at: tennis, swimming — and seducing.

I snuffed the Lucky in the dash ashtray, put away the Elgin, switched on the engine and rolled the Lincoln close to the entrance. I got out of the driver's door and stood there while an attendant opened the rear door for Mrs. A. Colin dutifully kissed his mother on her well-sculptured cheek.

"Mother, are you sure you don't want me to come with you?"

"Colin, go back inside and titillate some rich young thing."

"If that's an order . . ." Colin shrugged.

"It is. I'm going home, take off my shoes and have a double bourbon. Damn champagne makes me bilious." She looked at me and smiled. Oh, how the boys at the Copacabana must have reacted to that smile on other New Year's Eves. "Were you sufficiently bored, Alex?"

"I'm sufficiently paid not to be bored, Mrs. Alderdyce."

With a dancer's ease she slid into the limo

11

as Colin closed the door, but not before she could hear his dutiful directive to me.

"Take good care of her, Alex."

I tossed him a dutiful, "Uh-huh," took my place behind the wheel and shut the door without further comment. Colin strolled back toward the festivities and I glided the Lincoln across the driveway toward the iron gates of the estate.

I didn't despise Colin Alderdyce, it was just that I thought Mrs. A. was worthy of a better son — but then so was my mother.

A security guard thumbed an instrument attached to his belt and the iron gates swung open. As I sailed the limo through the pathway the guard smiled and saluted. The gates closed behind the Lincoln while the revelers within the glittering desert island guzzled champagne, safe and secure from snakes and other forms of would-be intruders into their stately pleasure-dome with walls and towers girdled round.

Scott Fitzgerald was right. The rich are different.

I cruised east on Palm Desert Road at about forty. I glanced into the rear view mirror and could make out her slim silhouette.

"Would you like me to turn on the heater, Ma'am?"

"No, thanks. I'm fine." Mrs. Alderdyce leaned forward a mite. "Alex."

"Yes, Ma'am."

"Told you don't call me 'Ma'am.' Call me Cyn."

"Yes, Ma'am."

"Stubborn bastard."

"Yes, Ma'am."

"Did I ever tell you that you remind me of my husband?"

"Yes, Ma'am."

"Well, you do. And that's the best I can say about any man. He went broke three times and each time ended up richer than before. He was a wildcatter. Independent. Insolent. But not with me. He was . . . well, never mind . . . but you'll find out that when you get old you start stumbling over your memories . . . just be sure you have something worth remembering."

"I'm working on that."

"I'll just bet." She pressed a button and the blue-coated divider window started to rise slowly. "I feel like being exclusive. Might even snooze for a couple of minutes — and dream about him. Play the radio if you like."

I switched the radio on to station KGRB out of West Covina. It plays music from the big band era. A little before my time. Glenn

13

Miller, Tommy Dorsey, Benny Goodman, Artie Shaw and all those other swingers. Shaw was the only one still alive and it happened they were playing one of his numbers, "This Time the Dream's on Me."

I wondered if Mrs. A. was dreaming about her husband, the wildcatter. An oilman out of Texas who made his last killing in the Kettleman Fields of California. A hard drilling, hard drinking giant who'd bet his last dollar on a hole in the ground or a hole card in a poker hand. Dream on, dear lady, dream on. I'll just bet you've got some things worth remembering.

Station KGRB segued from Artie Shaw's "This Time the Dream's on Me" to Nat King Cole singing "Night Lights." I looked up at the galaxies of nightlights millions of miles away, blinking down on this speck in space where another year had slipped into the eternal calendar. For me it hadn't been the best of years, nor the worst. I had banked a few bucks after paying cash for a "like-new" LeBaron convertible. I had received only minor injuries in the line of my chosen profession, mostly skinned knuckles along with the slings and arrows of unkept threats from irate adversaries. I had not heeded my mother's oft repeated advice to: A) get out of the private eye business, and

B) get married and have two sons and one daughter for whom she had already picked out names.

As I catalogued my pluses and minuses of the year I felt a growing discomfort, not mental, but physical. The shoulder holster cradling the .38 Special had slipped toward my armpit.

Instead of trying to adjust it while I was driving, I unbuttoned my jacket, slipped out the piece and placed it on the front seat. I looked into the rear view mirror. Mrs. Alderdyce was not in sight. For another half mile I followed the broken white line of the road until I became aware of the flashing lights from behind.

I switched to the exterior side view mirror. It was a black and white police car. The car with the flaring lights approached faster, intercepting the Lincoln, then pulled to a stop just off the road.

This maneuver had to be meant for me because there was no other traffic. The rest of the desert denizens were still at their respective parties or at home. I swung the Lincoln over and stopped a few yards behind the black and white.

I tucked the Police Special back into the shoulder holster and pulled the wallet with my driver's license from my back pocket.

The divider window glided down.

"What is it, Alex?" Mrs. Alderdyce inquired.

"Probably just a routine sobriety stop, Mrs. Alderdyce. Only take a minute."

"Damn!"

I pushed a button and the driver's window slid down. While I was talking to Mrs. A. I hadn't paid any attention to the approaching gendarmes. But now, just a fraction too late, I realized something was wrong: A) Cops don't usually stop limos for sobriety tests. B) Cops don't usually wear skin-colored ski masks. C) There was a .357 Magnum pointed at my brain.

Ironically, when I had turned the radio off Connie Boswell was singing "Say It Isn't So." My first inclination was to go for my gun. My second and almost immediate inclination was to dismiss my first inclination. When the cop with the Magnum leveled at my eyeball spoke, I could tell that he had a wad of something tucked in his mouth to disguise his voice.

"Unlock the doors."

"Right."

I pressed another button and there was an audible click.

The second cop jerked open the rear door. His voice was also disguised.

16

"Take off those jewels, lady, and hand them over. Quick!"

"You can have them," Mrs. A. replied, calm as a plate of potato salad. "Just don't get nervous."

The second cop juked his gun a few inches closer to her for emphasis.

"I said quick!"

I turned my head toward the back seat.

"Eyes straight ahead, Sport," said the cop with the gun pointing at me.

"Anything you say, officer."

"Shut up."

These two were not rank amateurs stumbling around in the dark. In my business you can tell the pros from the wannabes. They might not be real cops, but they were used to guns and to giving commands, and most likely used to having their commands obeyed. They sounded and acted like a couple of drill sergeants I used to kill in my dreams.

There was nothing to do, but to do as they said. And Mrs. A. was playing it smart. She took off the necklace and bracelet without wasted motion and handed them to the second officer, who had produced what looked like a velvet pouch.

I kept glancing up and down the road for any sign of approaching traffic. But what good would that have done? Nobody was going to give a second thought to a couple of cops who probably were handing out a speeding ticket. These boys were bright. They had picked out the ideal time and place, and the perfect guise with which to relieve an old woman of over a million dollars' worth of jewelry, while the moron who was supposed to protect her and the gems sat like a stuffed turkey in a dark oven.

The second cop dumped the jewelry into the bag and motioned with his gun to Mrs. A.

"Get on the floor and stay there!"

"Really!" Mrs. A. responded with regal indignation.

"Do it!"

She did. He slammed the door shut.

The first cop opened the driver's door, grabbed the front of my jacket along with some hair on my chest and came down hard across my skull with the barrel of the Magnum.

Instinctively I pulled back. The cop didn't deliver as true a blow as he might have but it was true enough to send a jolt of pain deep into my brain.

I mustered all my willpower struggling to stay conscious while giving the impression that I was dead in the water.

It could have been worse. He could have pulled the trigger.

My eyes yawned and through a blurry haze I saw the two cops head toward their car with the confident stride of a couple of linebackers.

As soon as they were in the black and white I made my move, even though my legs seemed to belong to somebody else. The cop car pulled away and I was wobbling out of the limo, wading through a block of Jell-O, toward the rear door. I managed to open it and grab at Mrs. A., who was nesting on the floorboard.

"Get out," I yelled.

"What!?"

"Get the hell out!"

She looked at me like I was nuts. Maybe I was. I pulled her out of the limo.

"Are you nuts?" She said it.

"Just stay here." I headed for the wheel.

"Alex, I forbid this."

"Yes, Ma'am."

I started the engine.

"Just a minute." She opened the door and reached into the rear seat.

I glanced at her for a second. She pulled something out of the back seat.

"My purse."

What a tomato, I thought to myself and

roared away as the back door banged shut leaving Mrs. A. standing clutching her evening bag on the shoulder of the road.

I didn't have an exact plan but I intended to make one up as I went along. I knew that I couldn't just sit there and have to explain to her, to the real police and to myself that I allowed this to happen without doing something about it. Sure, the jewels were insured and the insurance company would settle for whatever they were worth. But I had to settle with myself. With my stubborn Greek pride. Aristotle would probably have been philosophical about the whole situation, but his student Alexander the Great would have given pursuit. For all I know the blood of the mighty Macedonian is in my veins. If so, some of that blood was leaking from my skull into my left eye.

I wiped away Alexander's blood and floored the gas pedal. The Lincoln loved it — and damn it, so did I.

I managed to grab the phone from the arm rest and punch 9-1-1.

"This is an emergency," I barked at whoever responded. The respondent started to ask something but I cut her off. "Just shut up and listen. Alex Night, Private Investigator. Armed robbery in progress. Pursuing counterfeit cop car — repeat pursuing counterfeit cop car east on Palm Desert Road near Bob Hope Drive. Lincoln Limo pursuing counterfeit cop car east on Palm Desert Drive. Send help. Counterfeit cops are armed and dangerous. Send help!"

I slammed the phone back onto its cradle.

I could barely make out the taillights of the black and white a long way ahead. But the distance was diminishing. The Lincoln was a lot more powerful than the cop car. And so was I. At least I had to keep thinking I was.

It was time to talk back to the boys in blue. I took the Police Special out of my shoulder holster, switched it to my left hand and fired a couple of rounds out of the driver's window at the car ahead.

The black and white swerved but kept going. So did I. Right into a couple of gun blasts. One of the blasts spun an instant spider web on the right side of the Lincoln's windshield. The other slug went through the night air and landed I know not where.

But I was walking on their heels.

The limo's front bumper banged into the rear of the cop car and I heard the sweet sound of metal on metal and felt the jolting impact — once — twice — three times — but no strike out.

The black and white crossed the center

divider line onto the wrong side of the road. Me too.

I banged into the cop car harder and twisted the wheel. The cop car went out of control, careened into a ditch and crashed against a white concrete pillar.

The limo ended up in the same ditch but in much better shape. Somehow their headlights and mine stayed lit.

The two dazed cops staggered out, guns drawn, shooting in my direction. The second cop still managed to hold onto the velvet pouch.

By now the old adrenaline was pumping full bore. I opened the limo door and used it for cover. I fired and hit the second cop who dropped to one knee, shot back, then collapsed.

The first cop started toward his wounded comrade — and the velvet pouch on the ground. I aimed with both hands and fired again. The bullet creased the first cop's upper sleeve. He had enough. He turned and ran into the darkness. I let him go on his way. What I wanted he had left behind. The velvet pouch.

Gun still pointed, I walked slowly toward my quarry. I could see my picture in the newspapers as I held up the jewels with a modest Gary Cooper look on my face.

Heck, it wasn't anything that any self-respecting private eye wouldn't do. Well yes, I did put my life at risk against insuperable odds, but it was all part of the game. Sam Spade, Philip Marlowe and the other boys in the club had done it hundreds of times, I . . . I was suddenly startled out of my reverie.

The collapsed cop was no longer collapsed.

The sonofabitch sprang up and fired. I fired back, but not before I felt what seemed like a red hot rebar tear through my shin. I was ready to shoot again but his gun fell to the ground and so did he.

I waited for him to move again. But he didn't have any movement left. I reached down to my left leg. A bloody mess.

I breathed a few deep breaths then limped foreword toward the fallen sparrow. I picked up the sparrow's gun and tossed it a few feet away. Then I picked up the velvet pouch, only it wasn't velvet. It was chamois.

But the important thing was that it was heavy. I pulled open the draw strings and looked in. The jewelry glittered from the headlights. It was a sight to behold. A bloody sight at that. My blood, the blood of the fake cop at my feet and maybe some blood of the fake cop that got away.

It was time that I did something about the leak in my leg. I pulled the draw string closed on the chamois pouch, then reached into my back pocket and removed one of the monogrammed handkerchiefs that my mother had given me for Christmas a few years ago. I had never even wiped my face with it, but I put it to good use now. Merry Christmas, Mom.

I used the barrel of my revolver to fashion a tourniquet above the knee.

Then I sat and waited. I waited among the snakes and tortoises whom I could not see. If I had been thinking straight I would have crawled to the limo phone and called 9-1-1 again. But for some reason at that time that never occurred to me. I'm not really sure, maybe it did and maybe I dismissed the idea because it was too much trouble. Maybe I thought that the real cops were already on their way. But I was content to just sit there and daydream — even though it was night.

It's strange, the thoughts you think about when you daydream at night, sitting in the sand holding a tourniquet in one hand and a bag of jewels in the other.

People in my business — the detective business — spend a lot of time just waiting. You get used to it. And you spend the waiting time thinking about this and that.

This time I thought about Nick Charles. That's right, Nick Charles, Dashiell Hammett's last detective. Charles was the hero, if you can call him that, of Hammett's fifth and last novel. Mistakenly, he was referred to as "The Thin Man" because that was the name of the novel and the movie. The thin man in the story actually was a client of Nick's named Clyde Wynant — but the appellation stuck to Dash's detective and that's what he was called in all the sequels with which Hammett had nothing to do except collect royalties.

I guess I related to Nick Charles because not only was he a private investigator, but he was Greek. According to Hammett's story Nick's real name was Charalambides. It was anglicized to Charles by "that mug that put him through Ellis Island." So, while I didn't look anything like William Powell who portrayed him on the screen, I felt a certain kinship.

But where the hell was my Nora? Why couldn't I come across a beautiful redhead whose father was rich and had conveniently died and left her a lumber mill, a narrow gauge railroad and a fortune? If that ever did happen you could bet the farm that I'd take heed of my mother's advice to "quit this cockeyed business and get married."

I'd settle down with the perfect wife and pursue the perfect martini, instead of sticking my Grecian nose into other people's business while dodging bullets and chasing counterfeit cops.

Nora, my Nora where are you? All I ever come across is actresses and singers and screwy wives whose ideas of beauty and a good time are plastic surgery and dope. I was even engaged to one once. An actress. She thought the most important part of acting was spending three hours at the makeup mirror.

We never did get married. Not to each other. But she did, twice since then and now she's engaged again — but not to me. Me, I'm still looking for Nora.

Maybe it was from loss of blood. Maybe I was just cracking up, but I still have a clear recollection of standing up that night in the desert, facing the Santa Rosa Mountains while clutching the tourniquet with one hand and the chamois pouch with the other and hollering, "Nora! Nora!" Like Heathcliffe on the Heights. "Nora, I'm here waiting. Where are you, Nora?!"

That's when out of the darkness I saw and heard something approaching. Not Nora.

It turned out to be two police cars, lights flashing, sirens wailing. A couple of spotlights beamed at me and I stood there like a frozen rabbit.

Doors flew open. Several officers exited the cars with their guns pointed. I thought the bastards were going to shoot me.

I managed to raise a hand. The hand with the pouch.

"Take it easy fellas. Don't want to get hit with friendly fire."

They still weren't sure.

Then I heard her voice and saw her. Mrs. Alderdyce ran out of one of the police cars. She was still clutching her purse. I never saw anything more beautiful in all my life.

"It's all right, officers," she said, pushing one of the cops aside and running up to me, close enough so I could smell her expensive perfume. Chanel, I think it was. She put her hand on my bloodstained face. "Alex. God! Are you all right?"

"Still kicking," I said. "With one leg."

"You dumb sonofabitch." She smiled.

"Yes, Ma'am," I replied.

One of the cops had been examining the fake cop on the ground.

"This one's still alive," the real cop said.

"Shouldn't be," I said.

The real cops scrambled around in an effort to do what they could for the wounded man. They didn't seem to be doing a hell of a lot for this wounded man. At least that's how it appeared to me. But I did hear one of the cops on the squawker calling for an ambulance.

"Give me back my jewels," said Mrs. A., pointing to the pouch.

"Yes, Ma'am." I managed to lift the pouch. She took it.

"Alex . . ."

"Yes, Ma'am?"

"Happy New Year."

The whole thing seemed screwy. It made as much sense as going on an archaeological dig and finding your own bones.

Chapter Two

There's a song that goes, "Why, oh why, did I ever leave Ohio?" There are times when I think about the question that that song poses. But the answer comes quick enough. If you had been in Akron, the tire capital of the world, when I was, you'd know the answer.

There was the perpetual stench of burning rubber, the fumes that made breathing a constant challenge. There were my boyhood friends on Fink Street whose hobby was mugging and whose ambition consisted of making good use of the latex products manufactured by companies called Trojan and Sheik.

But then again, maybe I should have toughed it out. Most of the tire companies are closed. Most of my Fink Street friends are in jail, or dead. The only thing that seems to be thriving is the condom companies. Chalk one up for safe sex.

My dad, John Night, owned a saloon, respectable as bars go. It was a tavern where working men hung out. There were a few women, whom the men in those days called "Haybags" — but as bars go, respectable. You could get a bet down on basketball, baseball, football — a respectable bet. Hell, even cops came by for a free drink and to put a couple of bucks down on the Indians and the Browns.

John Night was honest — and tough. In my mind's eye I can still see him. If anybody got out of line, he'd get a warning from John. Once, maybe twice. Never three times. The third time, John Night was over the bar pulling off his glasses with one hand and throwing a punch with the other. That's all it ever took.

He married a Greek girl named Euridice Mulopolous who came to America after WW II. They had a son, me, and lived happily ever after until John sold the saloon and they moved to Miami. He died of a heart attack three months later at the age of fifty six. He had never been sick a day of his life and had survived three landings in the not-so-Pacific during the forties.

Today they would have given him a new heart. But he couldn't wait for science to catch up.

I left the ugly environs of Akron and went west, all the way to Vietnam, but that's another chapter in another story. After my peace mission to the Far East, I settled in Los Angeles and took up a cushy job with the Police Department. They had more rules than the Army so I went to work for myself where I could make up my own rules, more or less.

Most of my clients were in what is called "show business." You could read their names in *Variety* and *The Hollywood Reporter*. Part of my time was spent keeping their names out of police reports and courtrooms — movie and television people, singers, dancers, rock stars, producers, directors and writers.

When they were in trouble they all seemed to gravitate to A. Night over on Larchmont and Beverly. In the last fifteen years I'd gotten to know my way around — or through — all sorts of trouble. One thing I learned was to stay away from divorce cases. Once I let myself get hired by a female client whose director husband was cheating and beating on her. I got the goods on him on both counts. But they reconciled. She refused to pay me and he sued me.

But I've taken on just about anything — from finding celebrities' runaway kids to making sure sex symbols stay sober and celibate on location. I've worked for studios, networks, record companies — even did

31

jobs for Max Factor a couple of times — and, like the Johnny Mercer song, making a monkey look good.

My mother hated Florida almost as much as she hated Akron. So after my dad died, that left her only one place to go. She's been out here over four years, mending my socks and trying to get me to mend my ways. But we don't live in the same house. She bought a duplex on Van Ness near St. Brendan's Church, lives downstairs and rents out the upstairs.

Just think, I was thinking to myself as I lay in the hospital — only a few hours ago you called your mother to tell her you were in Palm Springs and to wish her a Happy New Year. Only a couple of hours ago you were trading bullets with a couple of strangers and now here you are, all bandaged up nice and safe and tucked in at a Palm Desert hospital. Happy New Year, Mr. Night.

It all defied probability. But it just goes to prove that something can defy probability and still be possible.

The hospital was a four story sort of Spanish-type building on an inlet between Palm Desert and LaQuinta. The operating rooms and Intensive Care were on the fourth floor. My accommodations were on the third floor.

It was pleasant enough, although I've spent many more pleasant New Year's nights in various places from Akron to Zagreb. But I was still alive and as well, or better off, than most of my enemies, as I rested there wardrobed in hospital gown, left leg propped higher than the right. The ride in the ambulance had been uneventful. There was a doctor whose face I was unable to recall and his faithful companion, a nurse whose features also eluded my memory.

Somebody had given me a shot of something — from a needle — not a glass, and then there was some stitchery performed on my gam after somebody else shaved the shin area. A journey by gurney brought me to the rest and recuperation room on the third floor.

The drumbeat in my brain had tempered into a muffled tom-tom, as I lay there, dying for a cigarette. The doctor and nurse walked in. How could I have forgotten what they looked like? It all came back to me when they re-entered my life.

He looked like Boris Karloff. But he lacked Karloff's compassion. She looked like Oliver Hardy, except her mustache was wispier. But then again, what the hell could I expect in the emergency room on New Year's night — Gregory Peck and Ingrid Bergman?

"Do you feel up to a little company, Mr. Night? They've been waiting all this time," the doctor spoke.

"They?" I inquired. I figured Mrs. A. would have stuck around. She was that type. But who else?

"Mrs. Alderdyce and her son. She called him right after she got here."

"Sure. Shoo 'em in, Doc. Shoo 'em in."

The doctor nodded to the nurse. She moved toward the door — rather gracefully, I thought, for Oliver Hardy.

"Thanks, Doc," I pointed to my leg and bandaged head, "for the repair job. By the way, what is your name? We never did get introduced."

"Penzer. Otto Penzer."

"Glad to know you, Dr. Penzer. Can I smoke?"

"Best you don't."

"I know that, but can I smoke?"

"No."

"You and the damn Surgeon General."

I could have added my mother to the company of anti-cigarette conspirators, but that wouldn't have meant much to Otto Penzer so I didn't bother.

The nurse re-entered, followed by Mrs. Alderdyce and son. But they were followed by two unannounced guests. Mrs.

Alderdyce was still wearing her gown and had put her jewels back on. The night's events had left her unmarred. She looked as regal and elegant as she did at Walter Annenberg's ball. Colin was still tuxedoed and tan.

Mrs. A. walked close to my bed and frowned.

"Alex, I'll never forgive you . . ." The frown segued into a smile and she pressed my hand, ". . . or forget what you did." She let go of my mitt and turned to the medicine man. "Dr. Penzer, how badly is he damaged — besides the brain?"

Dr. Penzer stepped forward and surveyed me, then spoke as if he were delivering an autopsy report.

"Well, the brain did suffer a slight concussion. Moving south — a couple of cracked ribs. A chipped shin bone from a .357 slug. The slug also went through an artery, causing quite a loss of blood. The blood has been replaced. The artery repaired. The bone will heal. The patient will limp for a time."

"I've always thought," said I, "that a limp made a man seem . . . mysterious."

"The trouble with you," Colin smiled, "is you don't know when to give up."

"He doesn't know how to give up,"

chimed Mrs. Alderdyce.

"Alex," Colin sounded as sincere as I had ever remembered. "I want to personally thank you . . ."

"Colin," I interrupted. "You're personally welcome. Doc, you sure I can't smoke?"

"You can smoke," said Dr. Otto Penzer, and I brightened until he added, "you can drink, you can eat an alligator — and then you can collapse and remain here until you come to your senses, or you can follow doctor's orders."

"Yes, master," I replied.

At that point one of the two unannounced guests stepped forward. He was obviously in command of the duet. He produced a pad and a lead pencil — a Parker Cross Hatch with a military clip. I had seen this kind of cop before. Precise. Meticulous. Boring.

"Mr. Night," he spoke in a clipped, officious tattoo. "I'm Lieutenant Louis Wax, Palm Desert Police Department."

"Yeah, you would be," I nodded.

Wax gave Dr. Penzer a perfunctory professional look, "I'll be brief, Doctor."

"Appreciate it," said Dr. Penzer.

Lt. Wax referred to his pad, then to me.

"You are Alexander Night. Private Investigator. Los Angeles . . ."

"Check and double check," I confirmed.

". . . hired by Mrs. Alderdyce to escort her and protect a million dollars in jewels . . ."

"Two million," Colin corrected.

"Two million," Wax continued. "On Palm Desert Road you were stopped by a pair of bogus police officers. The jewels were taken. You proceeded to give chase . . ."

"Oh yeah," I said. "I give good chase."

"A gunfight ensued," Wax went on. "One of the bogus officers escaped. The other was wounded. So were you. And the jewels were recovered."

"Just that simple," I looked at Dr. Penzer. "How's Bogus number two?"

I thought I saw ol' Otto almost smile.

"It appears he'll recover. But not as quickly as you. He's out of the operating room." Dr. Penzer had had enough of the inquisition. So had I. Penzer cleared his throat dismissively and spoke to Wax. "Uh, Lieutenant Wax, if you don't mind . . ."

Wax closed the pad and inserted the Parker inside his vest pocket. I noticed that the lip of the pocket had been worn threadbare from much insertion and extrusion of the writing instrument.

"I guess the rest can wait," Wax consented, then looked at me. "Goodnight, Mr. . . . Night."

"Happy New Year, Mr. Wax." I shifted my attention to the other cop. "Nice talking to you, Mr. Foozle."

Wax and Foozle, or whatever his name was, went out the door. I can't say I was sorry to see them depart. Matter of fact I wanted everybody to depart. I wanted to dream about my favorite redhead — Nora.

"Colin," I suggested, "take your mother and the jewels home. It'll soon be daylight."

"Alex is right, Mother," said Colin dutifully.

"All right," Mrs. A. nodded.

"I'd also advise you to take off those sparklers, Mrs. A. and put them in a safe haven."

"We'll call you, Alex," she said and moved toward the door.

"Make it late. I'm getting dopey."

"Goodnight, wildcatter," she smiled, and they were gone.

I thought to myself, they don't make them like that anymore. Tough as a timber wolf, but all woman. What a siren she must have been. She could still whistle the birds out of their trees. That night she'd been robbed, manhandled and browbeaten, but when she walked out of there she was as cool and calm as a lily pond.

Dr. Penzer was looking straight at me. I

thought I'd give it one more try.

"Doc, just one little . . ." I motioned two fingers toward my mouth. The phone rang. Penzer reacted as if he'd been goosed by an electric prod.

"Nurse, I left instructions — no phone calls!" Nurse Oliver didn't react nearly as much as the doctor. She didn't seem to have been goosed by anything. She probably never had been. She picked up the phone and spoke with a light voice for such a heavy person.

"I'm sorry, Doctor's orders. This room can receive no . . . oh . . ."

A pause as she listened and looked at Dr. Penzer.

"Oh, I see. Just a moment, please. Doctor, it's a Lieutenant Carter, Beverly Hills Police. He insists . . ."

"Garter," I corrected. "Lieutenant Detective, Myron Garter. Let me have it."

The nurse looked to the doctor. Dr. Penzer shrugged. By now he was probably past caring. She handed me the phone.

Myron Garter was my best friend. It's a good idea to have your best friend be a member of some police department, especially if you're a private investigator. The more prominent the member, the better. Lieutenant Garter was prominent in more ways than one. First in rank, then in weight. He looked like William Conrad in *The Killers* or *Body and Soul*, before Conrad put on a lot more stones and became Frank Cannon, then the fat man in *Jake and the Fat Man*.

Myron wasn't nearly as fat as Bill Conrad, still, the top button and buttonhole in Garter's shirt could never quite converge. He had put on more than fifty pounds in the last couple of years from overeating. The police psychologist told him that he was trying to compensate for the loss he had suffered.

What Garter lost was his wife. No, she hadn't died. But she and the Coldwell Banker real estate salesman Myron caught her with in *flagrante-delicto* were both lucky to escape with their naked skins intact.

Rhoda and Myron had been happily married for nearly eighteen years. You never know what goes on in the house next door. Myron didn't know what was going on in his own house. I knew. Maybe I should have told him.

"What's the matter, Myron?" I said into the phone. "Couldn't you get a date for New Year's Eve?"

"Matter of fact I do have a date — let you talk to her in a minute."

"If you're looking for a bet on the Rose

Bowl, I'll take UCLA and . . ."

"Not funny," he said.

"Then don't laugh," I said. "How did you find me, Myron? You got a snitch in Palm Desert?"

"No, I got crystal balls — everywhere."

I was not getting many points in the game of "Can You Top This?" that we were playing. On an even field I could always beat him in the riposte department, but tonight I was at a disadvantage, what with bullet holes, bruises and lack of nicotine and alcohol. He was probably puffing on an El Producto and sipping brandy.

"Myron, if you called to give me aggravation . . ."

"Oh, no, Alex, I'm not going to give you aggravation. But somebody is. Here's your MOTHER, Alex."

That was a shocker.

The last person I wanted to deal with tonight, or this morning, was my mother. I had gone and done it again. Given her fodder for her favorite Philippic.

I braced myself for the coming broadside.

"Alex . . ."

"Uh, Happy New Year, Mom."

"Never mind the olive oil."

I had heard that phrase before. A hundred times. A hundred times a hundred times.

41

From pre-puberty to post-meridian. Whenever she caught me with my pants down, figuratively and sometimes literally. For decades. From the time I was baptized at Holy Trinity, to last Thursday I think it was, she had found occasion to utilize that classic phrase.

"Alex," she went on. "What are you trying to do?"

"Do, Mom?"

"Alex, listen to me . . ."

As if I had a choice.

". . . I want to die before you do."

"Take it easy, Mom."

"Don't give me the easy. Alex, get out of this cockeyed private eye business before I have to bury you."

"I intend to be cremated."

"This year?"

She had me and she knew it. And she knew I knew it. I had to call off this conversation before I made another filial promise I had no intention of keeping. This time I had the perfect out. She knew I was in a hospital. Use strategy I said to myself, but before I could deploy, she was at it again.

"Where were you shot?"

"In the desert."

"You know what I mean. How are your organs? Can you have children?"

"They never touched my organs. You'll be a grandmother before you get another gray hair."

"You've given me enough already."

"Grandchildren?"

"Gray hairs, Alex . . ."

"Look Mom. I got to hang up now." Then I deployed my hospital strategy. "Doctor's orders. But don't worry. I'll call you tomorrow."

"If you live that long."

"Mom, I'm perfectly safe. I'm in a hospital. What could possibly happen?"

If I'd only known. If I had had one of Lieutenant Garter's crystal balls, I could have seen murder.

But that night, after Dr. Penzer and the lady in white left, I didn't want to see anything.

I was content to float on a cloud of tranquility. There had been damn little tranquility in my life. Not on Fink Street. Not in Vietnam. Not on the LAPD. Not in the benighted profession of a private investigator in Hollywood.

For now, all I wanted was, as the song says, "To leave it all behind — and go and find" — Nora.

In her arms there would be surcease,

maybe even success. If things worked out, I would cuckold Nick Charles and add adultery to my trespasses.

Chapter Three

Things didn't turn out the way I expected in my dreams. Or at the hospital.

In my dreams Nora never did show up. Evidently she and Nick were still happily married. So I went to the Annenberg party — in my dream. This time I wasn't dressed as a chauffeur, waiting in the driveway.

I was inside the mansion and inside a tuxedo. The place had more marble columns than the pristine Parthenon.

The usual crowd was there. Some of them who are still alive and some of them who aren't. But in a dream you can't tell the living from the dead.

Sinatra and the entire Rat Pack. Bogart, Bacall, Lawford, Garland, Sammy, and Dean Martin.

There were Ronnie and Nancy. Liz looked voluptuous.

I mingled, treating them all as equals. I felt obliged to dance with Zsa Zsa since no one was paying her any attention. After the dance I bowed graciously and turned my attention to a tray of truffles.

Les Brown and His Band of Renown alternated sets with Paul Whiteman. The vocalists included Doris Day and Madonna.

I spent a few secret moments with Meryl Streep and then moved on to Esther Williams who wore a bathing suit type evening gown.

Just before midnight Cynthia Alderdyce asked me to dance with her. But she was young and beautiful, with raven black hair, a figure right out of the chorus line of the Copa.

We swirled together as I held her close in my arms while Guy Lombardo played "Auld Lang Syne" and just at the stroke of midnight I was wearing a chauffeur's outfit again, driving Miss Daisy — only it was Cynthia Alderdyce sixtysomething again and the blue-coated divider window was rising slowly — then a slow motion montage with ski-masked cops pointing guns.

One of the guns cracked my skull, then I was dragging Cynthia Alderdyce out of the car and giving chase to the counterfeit cops —

Bullets blasted the windshield — and bumpers banged together — a crash — more gunfire — an enemy went down — Charlie? — no that was another war —

The counterfeit cop — but I was bleeding.

And then I stood in the desert cove and called out to the Santa Rosa Mountains — "Nora!" "Nora!" "Nora!" "Nora!"

Silence.

Then the answer.

A siren.

Another siren.

In my dream I heard sirens.

The sirens in my dream woke me up.

But the sirens weren't a dream.

They were real.

They were responding to a murder.

Chapter Four

Outside the Palm Desert Hospital there was a tape outlining the spot where the body had landed. By now the body had been removed.

But there were orange rubber stanchions rimmed with plastic yellow ribbons emblazoned with:

POLICE LINE — DO NOT CROSS

Several police officers and police vehicles were in evidence.

I was still inside the hospital and still in bed. Once again I had visitors. The faces were familiar. Besides Dr. Penzer who looked as if he had not gone to sleep, there was his faithful nurse who looked as if she hadn't lost any weight. Also present were Lieutenant Louis Wax and the silent one.

"What the hell happened?" I felt I had a right to know.

Wax rubbed his bony cheek with the clip end of his Parker pencil. He seemed in no hurry to respond to my question. But in his own good time he did.

"Well, somehow the suspect, who was also the victim, got to the roof . . ."

"Bogus number two?"

"Yes."

"Go on."

"He got to the roof and dropped to his death below."

"Hold it. Hold it! Let's take this fairy tale one step at a time. In the first place why didn't he drop out of his own window?"

"The windows are sealed." Wax shrugged.

"So I noticed. Now. In the second place do you for one misguided minute believe that a guy ventilated by two .38 slugs gets out of bed, walks to the roof and commits suicide?"

"Well . . ."

"Well, your ass." I looked toward Otto Penzer. "Doctor?"

"It does not appear possible."

"You bet your bedpan. Lieutenant Wax, it appears that you've got a slight case of murder here."

"Yes. So it appears."

"Well," I said. "Go ahead and solve it."

"Night, did you see or hear anything at all after we left?"

There wasn't any point in telling Wax

about my dream. Maybe my analyst could make something out of it. If I had an analyst.

"No Lieutenant. Not 'til the wake-up call from your sirens." I shifted back to the doctor. "Doc, what about security? Don't you people have a security force in this place?"

"One man at night," Penzer shrugged. "It's relatively easy for somebody to get in and out without being detected."

"That's just what somebody did, and left some dirty laundry behind. Maybe he tried to make it look like suicide, maybe he didn't much care. But what we're left with is a suspect who might have talked about a robbery, who turned into a victim who's through talking about anything."

There was a moment of silence in the room. Wax gave his bony cheek one last rub then slipped the Parker back into its threadbare scabbard.

"Lieutenant Wax," I broke the silence.

"Yes?"

"Did you get an I.D. on the suspect — victim?"

"He carried nothing on his person that would identify him."

"Scars? Tattoos? Extra fingers or toes?"

"Only a ring."

"What kind of ring?"

"Wedding."

"So somewhere there's a grieving widow."

"We'll I.D. him alright. His prints are already on the computer."

"Too bad you can't find some prints of the guy who tossed him over — hey, did you try?"

"We're working over the remains and the whole hospital."

"Well, it could've been worse."

"What do you mean?" Wax asked.

"It could've been me," I answered.

In the next four days while I stayed in the hospital, the slight case of murder remained unsolved. With Wax on the case the boys back at John's Bar in Akron, Ohio would have bet heavily on the murderer. So would I.

Meantime, as I watched my favorite movie channel, American Movie Classics, I was going through nicotine withdrawal — cold turkey. AMC plays old movies. Did you ever notice that in all those old movies everybody smokes . . . and smokes? Men and women. Wayne, Gable, Garfield, Bogart, Lancaster, Kirk Douglas, Paul Henried — hell, Henried lit them two at a time, one for him and one for Bette Davis. And all those other glamorous dames, Garbo, Harlow, Hedy Lamarr, Rita Hayworth, Hepburn — Katharine and Audrey — hell, everybody smoked, even minors like the Dead End Kids, Tom Sawyer and Huck — smoking, all of them, everywhere, bedrooms, boardrooms, bars, basements — all of them walking, talking, laughing — smoking, in love and war.

Sherman said that war is hell. I don't agree completely. At least in war you can smoke.

In a monastery you can smoke.

In a prison you can smoke.

But not in that damn hospital.

I even found myself wooing Nurse Oliver. Hardy's nickname was "Babe." I tried calling her that and more. I more than implied that if she'd sneak me some Luckies . . . but the implication was rebuffed. Cary Grant or Hugh Grant could not have melted her. She wasn't Oliver Hardy. She was Oliver Stone.

I was rescued by Cynthia Alderdyce, when that dear, sweet, saintly woman came to visit; without my even asking her, she slipped me a pack of Luckies. I savored every puff. Smoked each clean white cylinder until it seared my lip.

What about the ashes, you might be wondering? Ah, ha. Mixed with a mastery of an alchemist among the remains from my food plates. Mixed and mashed until they were no longer discernible to the naked eye. And thus did I maintain my sanity among the Philistines.

And then there were the calls from my mother. When will some heir to Edison perfect the mute button for a telephone? But she really was quite reasonable about the whole situation, especially after I agreed to let her drive me home when I was discharged.

In the meantime, I watched more old movies on AMC, daytime — nighttime, sunrises — sunsets, and from my third-story window, the view of greater Palm Springs.

Palm Springs. It took only Bugsy Seigel to invent Las Vegas via the Flamingo. But it took three people to invent Palm Springs. Charlie Farrell and Ralph Bellamy, along with an assist from Humphrey Bogart, planted the seed with the Racquet Club in what was little more than an Indian Reservation in Palm Springs proper.

From that seed there blossomed Cathedral City, Rancho Mirage, Palm Desert, Indian Wells and LaQuinta. But the pilgrims call it all Palm Springs. Some years back, Palm Springs proper hit the skids, on account of kids — high school and college — particularly around Easter week; but also on other occasions when students, some stoned, some drunk, some celebrating the sexual revolution, some just for the hell of it, invaded the city and occupied sidewalks, streets, byways and buildings with automobiles, motorcycles, skateboards and rollerblades.

They wore very little clothing, sometimes none at all — went about buck naked. I never did know the difference between naked and buck naked. Either way, they disrupted traffic, tourists, citizens and shopkeepers. The city's reputation, infrastructure and economy took a nose-dive until the city fathers, mothers and, of all people, Mayor Sonny Bono, carried on a campaign enforced by a persuasive police department, whereby the infantile offenders were diffused, disseminated and dispersed.

There's quite a revival in the little ol' town what with new shops, malls, the museum, the annual Film Festival, and even the Palm Springs Walk of Stars along Palm Canyon Drive, Tahquita Canyon Way and Museum Drive. I even went down there to watch my old pal George Montgomery — who once played Philip Marlowe in *The*

Brasher Doubloon — get his star in front of the museum back in 1995.

The nearby Indian — make that Native American — gambling reservations haven't hurt the Palm Springs economic resurgence either.

Progress.

Speaking of progress, the time came when Dr. Penzer thought that I had made enough progress to leave the premises.

I made all the necessary arrangements before checking out, starting with Blue Cross and a few phone calls.

There had been a story in the *Los Angeles Times* about my little escapade. The amateur who wrote it missed his chance at a Pulitzer Prize by downplaying the whole thing. Still I had been getting quite a few messages on the office answering machine congratulating me and wishing me a speedy recovery. There were a few who took the opposite point of view. I made a list of those meriting a response.

I called Mrs. A. and Lieutenant Wax and told them both I'd keep in touch.

And then I called my mother to come and get me.

Chapter Five

There were just a few puff clouds in the otherwise clear blue Palm Springs sky as we were moving west toward Los Angeles on Highway 10. On both sides I could count at least six ranges of snow-studded mountains.

As we approached Whitewater, the landscape on both sides was lined with countless metal skeletons topped with three blades. Some of the blades were swirling, most were stationary. These intrusive objects sticking obscenely out of mother nature were power generators of some sort. They were also baldface blots on God's earth. Someone had told me that the owners received tax credit from the government, that the whole set-up was a scam; maybe yes, maybe no. But whatever else it was — it was plain ugly.

Another thing about them that bothered me was that with those three blades the whole thing looked like an elaborate advertisement for Mercedes-Benz.

At the time the three of us were cruising along in an American car, my mother's dark blue Jeep station wagon. There were three of us because my mother had brought along my favorite lieutenant of detectives to help deliver my body back to The City of the Angels.

Back at the hospital it had been a touching farewell as I shook hands with Dr. Penzer and kissed Nurse Oliver. For a mad moment I thought of doing it the other way around.

As memento of my stay at the medical facility I had taken with me a pair of metal crutches. I would have preferred a set of the old fashion wooden ones but I guess they went out of style without my noticing.

Actually, my stay at the hospital had been short, but too long. I don't like hospitals. There's something unhealthy about them. Especially that one.

My mother was at the wheel. She took to it like Paul Newman. She was born to drive. In the course of her myriad voyages my mother had succeeded in breaking every law in the books. Speeding. Tailgating. Stop signs. Red lights. She violated laws that haven't been invented. And yet, there must have been an angel on her shoulder. Not only had she never been in an accident — although she probably caused a few — she never so much as got a ticket. Not even for parking. While I . . . I, a driver exemplar, had suffered the humiliation of driving school twice within the last eighteen months. They were both bum beefs.

Lieutenant Myron Garter — who had done nothing to help get those tickets fixed — sat in the front seat of the Jeep nibbling a Snickers bar. I occupied the rear seat, left leg straight out, with the metal crutches as my companions.

But best of all, since leaving the hospital, I was smoking my third Lucky. Despite the air conditioner, the atmosphere was pleasantly clouded with a bluish haze and piquantly perfumed with the fragrance of nicotine. Free at last. Free at last!

We were approaching a small oasis between Cabazon and Apache Pass that harbored an enterprise featuring a huge sign:

HADLEY'S ORCHARDS
Food — Fruits — Wine — Date Shakes

The sign did not fail to catch the lieutenant's attention.

"Anybody hungry?" Garter inquired, as casually as he could.

"We'll eat when we get to my house." My mother highballed straight past Hadley's without a hint of hesitation. "I'll make

Avgolemonou soup."

She thought she was pulling a fast one. Well, as Bogart said in *High Sierra*, "I don't like fast ones." And I had no intention of letting her get away with it. I would draw the line in the desert sand while we were doing seventy-five.

Even though I loved Avgolemonou soup — a Greek dish made with rice, eggs and chicken — I was not about to be held hostage in a world I never made.

"We're not going to your house," I said.

There was an audible pause as the atmosphere grew thicker. Garter used the time to bite off the end of an El Producto and light it.

"We're going to my place," I finally concluded.

"No we're not," this time she snapped back immediately. "You're staying with me until you get well."

It was time for decisive action, and I was just the boy to take it. Shakespeare said, "There is a tide in the affairs of men . . ." For me, this was high tide. All or nothing at all.

I opened the rear door nearest to me. The car reacted as the door buffeted against the wind at seventy five. I could barely keep the damn thing ajar. My mother also reacted.

"Alex, what are you going to do?"

"Jump out."

"Go ahead. Jump." Both her hands were still on the wheel. She even picked up a little speed.

"Alex," Garter purred, a model of imperturbability. "Close the door."

"Who asked you?" I demanded.

"Jump," he shrugged.

For about half a mile it was a Greek standoff. Me with the door open. My mother with both hands on the wheel. Finally I spoke.

"Mom, I'm over twenty-one. A veteran."

"A veteran moron."

That exchange hadn't helped much.

"What a way to spend a day off," Lieutenant Garter observed.

I opened the door wider. I could see her looking in the rear view mirror.

"Good-bye." That was my valediction.

"Close the door," she said. "We'll go to your place."

Immediately I flipped the cigarette out of the Jeep and closed the door. Sweet victory.

It didn't take her long to figure out a way to save face.

"I don't want you smelling up my house with cigarette smoke anyhow."

I didn't feel it necessary to comment further. I savored my victory in silence — and by lighting another cigarette. But I knew there was something bothering my mother besides my cigarette smoke.

"You were bluffing," she finally said. That's what was bothering her.

"We'll never know," I replied trying not to be smug.

More silence. About a mile's worth. As we approached Banning she spoke again.

"I'm still making Avgolemonou soup."

As usual she got the last word in anyhow.

Chapter Six

"Robert Mitchum Dead," the headline screamed. The story, with pictures, was on the front page of the *Los Angeles Times*.

In my office I listened to a dead man talking. Sometime, during my absence and while he was close to dying, he had called and left a terse message on the answering machine. Mitchum's messages were always terse — and his voice unmistakable, a combination of caramel and ground pepper. This time his voice was a little coarser.

"Hello, you old dick. Heard about your misadventure — could have been worse — could've been hit in the vitals — speaking of 'worse' — I am — only this time I really mean it. Going to beat you to the barn — and what a ride it's been — *adios*."

That was one message I'd never erase.

I sat there and remembered a lot of things, including the "worse" story Mitchum told me a few years ago on the set of a picture he was working on called *The Old Dick*. Mitch was playing a retired private detective and I had been hired by the producer, who was a client of mine, to act as technical advisor.

Robert Mitchum needed a technical advisor on how to play a private dick like Aaron Spelling needed more space in his new house. But the producer owed me money and that way he could charge off my fee to the budget.

Back to the "worse" story. Years ago Mitchum came across Lex Barker in New York City. Barker had earlier played Tarzan and was built like a Viking.

"How are you, Lex?" Mitchum asked casually.

"I never felt better in my life," Lex answered.

The next day Lex Barker dropped dead. Since then Mitchum always answered, "Worse."

Needless to say I never presumed to give Mitchum any pointers on how to play a private eye. The others were all good. Bogart, William Powell, Dick Powell, Fred MacMurray, Dana Andrews, James Garner, Clint Eastwood, they all played cops and they were good, very good.

But Robert Mitchum was the quintessential private eye.

Mitchum's portrayal as Jeff Bailey in *Out*

of the Past is a masterpiece.

Howard Hughes once said to Mitchum, "Bob, you remind me of a pay toilet. You don't give a shit for nothing."

And that's the way Mitchum played it for years. Casual. Laid back. Languid. He was damn near ashamed of being an actor. But was he ever! Take a look at *The Story of G.I. Joe*, *Crossfire*, *Night of the Hunter*, *Heaven Knows, Mr. Allison*, *The Sundowners*, *Cape Fear* — the original. Mitchum had a secret. HE WAS AS GOOD AN ACTOR AS HE WANTED TO BE.

But what Robert Mitchum really wanted to be was — a writer. I'd read some of his stuff. Strong, sensitive and intelligent. Particularly his poetry. Mitchum had the I.Q. of a genius. But he rarely let it show.

I thought of his wife Dorothy. What a ride she had — and what a love story. The most beautiful women in the world went after Mitchum. Ava Gardner, Susan Hayward, Marilyn Monroe — a battalion of other beauties. But there was only one woman who could melt the Ice Man — Dorothy.

I'd have to call her later. But in the meantime, I played the message again and listened to that unforgettable voice.

Adios, old dick.

I was on the mend for the next couple of weeks. I didn't realize it for quite a while, but slowly an idea started to creep into my brain.

An idea that would change my life, for the better or worse. And like Fred MacMurray in *Double Indemnity*, I'm setting it down for the record — even if that record never sees the light of day. Even if I tear it up, or just let it lie in some dark, musty drawer. Because that idea — and the results — affected other lives, for better or worse, much worse.

There were times when my mother and Garter would come by and keep me company. She'd bring Avgolemonou soup. With Garter there, there was never any left over.

I took moderate exercise, walking with both crutches. After a while I traded them in for a couple of canes, like Everett Sloane in *Lady From Shanghai*.

I used the exercycle.

I took walks in the patch of a nearby park over on Beverly and Van Ness.

Part of the time I was on the phone. Mrs. Alderdyce called. I got the idea she was getting a little bored with the social season in Palm Springs.

I also got a few calls from some of my younger lady acquaintances. Most of them were bored with life. They were always looking for a little diversion. I wasn't up to the kind of diversion they were looking for, but promised to keep them posted. The time would soon come when I'd respond with alacrity to the lure of soft shoulders and dangerous curves.

I even took drives in the LeBaron with the top down. That's the great thing about a convertible in Southern California, you can drive all year long in half a car. And I watched old movies on television.

But mostly I read. And that's how the idea crept in. Because mostly I read detective stories. And mostly by Dashiell Hammett and Raymond Chandler.

I had read them before — *Red Harvest, The Dain Curse, The Maltese Falcon, The Thin Man,* and *The Big Sleep, Farewell, My Lovely, The High Window, Little Sister.*

I knew all the characters — the Operative, Sam Spade, Nick Charles and Philip Marlowe. I had the plots down pat. But this time I wasn't just interested in plot. I was studying character and style. And I was studying the authors, themselves.

I also took a fling at some of the younger hardboilers: Ambler, MacDonald, McBain and Parker — even Spillane.

But I always went back to the masters —

Hammett and Chandler — because there was a kinship between me and both of them — or maybe there would be.

That's when the idea became more than an idea.

I was down to one cane. I was getting restless. I even had a go with a set of soft shoulders and dangerous curves. Not quite up to par, but she didn't ask where the complaint department was.

You were right, Willie — "There is a tide in the affairs of men . . . !"

I was ready to spring it on somebody. Who else but Lieutenant Myron Garter and my beloved mother?

Chapter Seven

The setting was perfect. It was Sunday night and we had just watched my mother's favorite program, *Murder, She Wrote*, with Angela Lansbury.

I snapped off the television set. My mother sat in her favorite chair knitting me another scarf that I would never wear. She thought we were still in Akron, or that maybe I'd take a vacation to Nome or someplace else up north. I really don't know what she thought, except that I could use another scarf.

Lieutenant Myron Garter stretched out on his favorite couch. I only had one couch. He sipped a Glenfiddich scotch. He had given me the bottle for Christmas, knowing damn well that I don't drink scotch, and that he'd end up drinking the whole damn jug. As usual he was blowing smoke from an El Producto cigar.

I had planned the moment like a master showman. A production worthy of Ziegfeld or Yurok. Comfort, good food, drinks, a mystery movie and now the main event.

I lit a Lucky and took a few steps around the room, waving my Malacca idly as I began.

"Mom, I have something to say that's going to make you very happy."

"I'm going to be a grandmother?"

"Quit clowning, this is serious."

"So am I. I found two more gray hairs."

"You've got fewer gray hairs than I have."

"And a lot more common sense."

"Will you listen?"

"I think I'm going home," said Garter.

"Stay put," I said.

"Go ahead, Alex," my mother smiled. "Tell us what you're going to tell us."

"You want to stop knitting first?"

"No."

"Mom!"

"I can listen and knit. Talk."

"Okay. Mom, I'm finally going to take your advice."

"What advice is that? I forget."

"Holy Christ, Mom, what have you been asking me to do since you came to this town? Well, I'm going to do it. I'm going to quit the detective business."

My mother dropped a stitch. That's the first time I'd ever seen her do that.

Myron Garter choked on a chunk of cigar smoke.

By God I had gotten to both of them. But evidently Garter wanted to make sure.

"Say again," he said.

"Watch my lips. Quit-the-de-tec-tive-bis-ness."

"You hit the Lotto?" Garter asked when he had recovered.

"Nope."

"Thank you, Alex. I'll go to my grave happy — when I get ready to go." She resumed knitting, but added almost in the same breath, "But, uh, what are you going to do, son?"

Ah-ha, now for the second surprise. But I was in no hurry to spring it. I had both fish on my line and I was going to play both of them for a while before I gaffed them. They both leaned forward. I let them lean for a couple of beats, then:

"More important is what I'm not going to do. I'm not going to dodge any more bullets . . ."

"Some you didn't dodge," she pointed to my left leg.

"Right."

That night in Palm Desert wasn't the only time I came close to buying the farm. There was some shrapnel from Charlie bobbing around inside and a chunk of lead that had formed a permanent attachment near my spine in civilian life.

"I'm not going to shortchange any more undertakers," I said, then I went on to phase two. "Instead of risking my life, I'm going to write about suckers who risk theirs."

"A writer?" Garter exclaimed. "You're going to be a writer?"

"Damn right."

"You mean for those checkout counter magazines. Scandal sheets? Madonna? Michael Jackson? Babies with three heads?"

"Hell no. I mean mystery novels."

I walked over to a table and picked up a couple of books I had planted there earlier. One by Hammett, *The Maltese Falcon*, and one by Chandler, *The Big Sleep*. I held them both with one hand, spine out.

"Mystery novels, like in Hammett and Chandler."

"Oh, them," Garter exhaled some smoke.

"Yeah, them. We're a lot alike, 'specially Hammett and me."

"Such as?"

"Such as Hammett went to war. So did I."

"So did ten million other guys. Myself included."

"Dashiell Hammett was an investigator for the Pinkerton Detective Agency. He packed a gun before he started pecking at a

71

typewriter. Before he started writing short stories and then novels like *The Maltese Falcon*."

I set the *Falcon* back on the table.

"Sam Spade," Garter lisped.

"Chandler went bust in the oil business" — I held up *The Big Sleep* — "He was forty-five years old before he wrote his first novel and gave birth to Philip Marlowe."

"I'm glad somebody gave birth to something," my mother remarked.

"No more stakeouts; no more other people's dirty laundry; no more sneaking around pretending I'm somebody else; no more snapping pictures through bedroom windows . . ."

"No more paychecks," Garter cracked.

"I'll get by, wise guy. More than get by. This is a soft set-up. There's millions waiting to be made."

"He's serious." Garter sipped some Glenfiddich.

"You bet I'm serious. Hell, I'll be signing autographs in swank bookstores, traveling to New York, Chicago, St. Louis, Atlanta . . ."

"Skip Akron," my mother said.

"I'll be living in first class hotels, and you," I pointed to Garter reclining on the couch, "you, Myron Garter will still be crawling on your belly in some alley trying to make a bust. And if you do, the 'suspect' will be out in fifteen minutes thumbing his nose at you because you neglected to say 'excuse me, sir' when you caught him with a smoking gun."

"A slight exaggeration."

"I'm through with all of that; I'm getting out while I'm still alive and young enough to trade trades."

"What's the title of your first book, Alex?" my mother asked.

"I haven't thought about that yet. But I've got plenty of material to draw from. I've got a million stories with their tongues hanging out waiting to be written. If Hammett and Chandler did it, why can't I do the same thing?"

I put *The Big Sleep* back on the table and took a hit from the Lucky.

"Alex."

"Yes, Mom?"

"Why can't you quit smoking?"

Chapter Eight

There was something sticking in my craw. I'm not the tidiest fellow on the block. But I don't like leaving unfinished business. Especially in the detective business. At any other time in my life I would have gone after him. The temptation was still there. The bloodhound instinct was still strong. But I fought it.

I'm talking about the counterfeit cop in the desert. Bogus number one. I resented what he did. He made me unhappy. He hurt my tender sensibilities. He put a dent in my faith in mankind. And my head.

I don't like having a gun shoved in my face. It might have gone off. I don't like for my clients, especially a nice old lady, to be manhandled and robbed, even if I did get back the jewels.

I don't like being shot at.

There was a lot about that sonofabitch that I didn't like. And somewhere out there he was still on the loose. I wondered if I could ever make him in a lineup. Or on a street. Or a dark doorway. The odds were against it.

But he could make me.

Anytime, anyplace, he could step out of a staircase or into an elevator. He'd know me. But would I know him?

He spoke three sentences to me. I'll never forget them. You have a tendency to remember what a man says when he's pointing a gun at you.

First sentence: "Unlock the doors."

Second sentence: "Eyes straight ahead, Sport."

Third sentence: "Shut up."

I'd always wonder if he was the guy sitting next to me in a movie, or at a counter, or a football game.

It's a big, wide, wonderful world and chances are our trails would never cross — unless he wanted them to.

But why would he do that? I didn't have anything he wanted. Did I? I couldn't do him any harm. Could I?

The answer was no. He'd have no cause to come after me. Unless he thought I was going to come after him.

What could I do? Take out an ad in the paper saying, "Dear counterfeit cop — don't worry about a thing. I quit the detective business. Sleep warm — Regards A. Night."

Not likely.

I'd just have to play the odds and hope our trails would never cross. But that same something that stuck in my craw wanted exactly that to happen.

I kept telling myself that it was no longer my case. I didn't have any cases anymore. I was not a private investigator. I was a writer.

But old habits die hard. As I said, the temptation was still there. The bloodhound instinct was still strong. But I fought it. And I beat it.

The hell I did.

Chapter Nine

A. NIGHT
Private Investigator

That's what the sign on the frosted glass door said. But not for long. The letters were being scraped off by a professional sign painter who would then paint on a new inscription.

I stood there in the hallway, cane in hand, wearing Porsche sunglasses, watching as my former landlady was inside my former office with her future tenant going over the groundrules.

I hoped they would be happy together. She was a huge woman with hawkish features and he was a young psychologist with dandruff.

My stuff had already been moved out by the least expensive movers and storers I could find, aptly called "Cheapers, Creepers and Keepers." Part of it I stored, the other part was stuffed into my residence.

I had decided to give up my office on the corner of Larchmont and Beverly. Too many of my old clients would've continued to pester me there. I needed a change of venue. Besides Ms. Rat Lips was about to raise my rent again.

I looked at the steep stairway. A lot of memories had walked up and down those steps. Ladies with beautiful legs and ugly intentions, men with murder in their hearts, liars, cheats, swindlers — cowards and con men, sweethearts and stinkers.

By now the sign man had scraped my name off of the frosted glass.

Suddenly it hit me.

I was closing the door on the only way of life I'd known for over fifteen years. But as the old saying goes, "one door closes, another door opens."

I turned and made my way down the steep stairway with the support of my cane and the banister. For the first time in more than fifteen years I counted the number of steps. There were twenty-six.

Just as I counted step number twenty-six, the door opened and there stood one of the reasons I was moving away.

A client. No, an ex-client. Tawny Tucker. She looked like one of the beach girls on *Baywatch*, and she wasn't wearing a hell of a lot more than most of them. Her full moon breasts swayed uninhibitedly over a small circle of waist, valentined into healthy hips, then tapered down long, well-toned legs to tiny feet. She wore a spaghetti-strap dress consisting of just enough material to make a pillowcase. She also wore oversized sunglasses. Dark sunglasses.

The irony was that Tawny made most of her money doing voice-overs for commercials and cartoons. She could sound like anybody from Little Bo Peep to the Wicked Witch of the West. But once she got in front of the camera she practically froze stiff. There was something about being seen instead of just heard that tightened her every fiber and joint.

Tawny Tucker had spent a lot of paychecks and residuals on psychologists and psychiatrists but they couldn't untie or cut the knot that was caused by the camera — or something that happened a long time ago.

Knot or no, she was a good kid and I liked her.

"Oh, Alex, I was just coming up to your office to see you . . ."

"The office is closed."

". . . on business."

"And I'm out of business."

"Five hundred, Alex," her voice was pleading and it was no act. She wasn't reading lines or playing a part. She was scared, again. "If you'll just see Bennie . . . talk to him . . ."

I reached out and took the sunglasses from Tawny's face. Her left eye was bruised and swollen shut, again.

"I'll talk to you, Tawny, for the last time. Get away from that sonofabitch before he kills you." He was a part-time stripper at a joint on Bundy Drive.

"Alex . . ."

"If you want a second opinion, try the Battered Women's Hot Line."

I put the sunglasses back on her face, not too gently.

"Turn around and walk away, Tawny, from me and him."

She was crying, but she did turn around, open the door and walk away . . . from me. I didn't hold out much hope for the second half of my suggestion.

Bennie Fix was a good looking guy as guys go, with a good looking body as bodies go. He was good at using his good looks to charm the ladies, especially Tawny. He was also good at using his fists on women, especially Tawny. I don't know why she took it. But then again I don't know why any woman takes it. Something to do with self-esteem, I've been told. But then, I've been told a lot of things again and again. Psychiatrists have to listen. So do bartenders. So do private detectives, but now I was none-of-the-above.

Outside I stood for a moment in front of the door numbered 249 and looked up and down the boulevard at Larchmont Village. Things had changed in the last few years. Most of the small Mom and Pop shops had gone or were going out of business. In the old days there was only one sandwich shop, the Larchmont Deli; now there were a dozen new "in" restaurants, some even with tables and chairs on the sidewalk in a Parisian affectation of sorts. There was Louise's Tratoria, Prado Restaurant, B and L Patisserie, Café Chapeau, Gingham Garden, Café Pierrot, Girasole's, The Petite Greek and LaLuna and Koo-Koo Roo.

They'd have to sell an awful lot of meatballs, pork chops and pasta to pay the exorbitant rents. The landlords were turning the screws almost as tight as on Rodeo Drive in Beverly Hills.

One of the last old landmarks was gone. Landis Department Store had now become Hancock Savings run by a man aptly named Wolfus.

Other recent additions included Blockbuster Video, Jamba Juice and Noah's Bagels.

I was about to cut across the street when she walked around the corner. Another ex-client.

She was Frances Vale. A generation ago she was the sex queen of the flower generation. Heiress to a long line of sex queens — from Jean Harlow, to Betty Grable, Rita Hayworth, Marilyn Monroe, and then came Frances Vale during the sixties when "love" was in the air. So were napalm and pot.

The world was divided — half communist, half democratic. So was the USA: half hawks, half doves. The hawks wanted to make war, the doves wanted to make love. And they all wanted to make love to Frances Vale. A lot of them did.

I have to admit that a few years later I joined the club. She was a little past her prime then. She was past it even more now.

Still, she was some woman. Tall, still willowy, and still with the biggest, bluest eyes ever to smolder on the screen or off. They were smoldering right then. Nobody, even that day, ever passed by her without looking back. Her figure was a bit fuller, but sometimes fuller is better.

Today there are other sex queens, well maybe not queens, but some sort of royalty and quite a few pretenders, but put any of them up next to Frances Vale, turn the lights a little low, and even today, well . . .

"Hi, Alex. I was just coming to see you."

"Hi, Frances."

"Why don't you call me Franny?" She turned on those big blues. "The way you used to."

"Okay. I'll call you Franny. But not the way I used to."

"Say the rest of it."

"Fairest of the Rare, Rarest of the Fair," I said. That was the rest of it. I hadn't said it to her in a long time. I never thought I'd say it again.

"I heard you got hurt, Alex," she looked down at the cane. Her voice still had that Lorelei quality that I remembered on the screen and other places.

"I'm okay. How are you, Franny?"

"Let's go upstairs to your office. I've got to talk to you."

"Haven't got an office anymore."

"What's wrong, Alex? You need money, because if you do, just tell me how . . ."

"No, thanks, Franny. I'm fine in that department. I don't need any money."

I knew that she meant it. Franny was as generous as anybody I ever met. More generous, to everybody, except in certain ways, to herself. She had made a lot of money during her heyday. Ten box office hits in a row and her price practically doubled with each one. She even made records and albums. Sold millions. She had a nice, husky voice, couldn't carry a tune, but nobody cared. They just bought, especially the young flower people who wanted to grow up and be just like her. And posters, she even sold millions of posters wearing nothing but long straight blonde hair and a guitar. In spite of all her generosity, she still had most of her money, thanks to the honesty and loyalty of Mike Meadows, who used to be her agent and now ran Tri Arc Productions.

"Then how come you don't have your office anymore?"

"Because I don't need it. I quit the detective business. I switched to another line."

"What?"

"Don't laugh, Franny, but I'm going to be a writer."

"Laugh? Hell, Alex, I know you." The way that she said it sounded strange — and intimate. "You can be any damn thing you put your mind to."

"Thanks, Franny . . ."

"But, Alex, I want to talk to you . . . to hire you."

"I'm sorry, Franny. But I got to quit cold

turkey. Cut all ties." I pointed upstairs to where my office used to be. "I've just closed up shop."

"Alex, walk across the street with me. Have a cup of coffee. Please. For old times?"

"Okay."

We walked across the street to the B and L Patisserie, sat at one of the outside tables and ordered coffee. Even in the sunlight, in spite of all the dope and booze and God only knows what else, her face was unlined except for a few crinkles around the eyes and that beautiful mouth. Even her throat was smooth and tight. Maybe she had had some work done. If she did, it worked.

"What're you looking at, Alex, old times?"

"You look great, Franny."

"I been straight for years. No shit, no pot, no booze. Straight as Robin Hood's arrow."

"Good for you, Franny."

"It wasn't easy. There were times when I thought the walls would come tumbling down — and so would my head. It wasn't easy but I did it. I do look good don't I, Alex?"

"You look good. Fairest of the Rare. Rarest of the Fair."

"Tell that to that son of a bitch."

"What son of a bitch?"

"Mike."

"Mike Meadows?"

She nodded and sipped her coffee.

"Franny, there're a lot of son of a bitches in this town. Mike Meadows is not one of them. And you know that better than anybody."

"Not anymore I don't. You know what he talked me into? Had me sign the goddamn papers and everything."

"What?"

"A part in his goddamn lousy picture. Part? Shit, more like a bit, about three scenes playing a goddamn hundred-year-old mother to some snot-ass television actress I wouldn't let stand in for me if she was the only other woman left with me in the world."

"Who's the television actress?"

"What's the difference?"

"Who is it?"

"Jackie Mathews . . ."

"Franny, Jackie Mathews has made three big pictures, hasn't done television for years. She's a star."

"Never was a star. Isn't a star now. Never going to be a star. A lousy TV actress and he wants me to play her hundred-year-old goddamn drunken mother. I don't need that shit!"

She said it loud. Too loud. People sitting near us and walking on Larchmont turned and looked, and not because she was beautiful.

"So what do you want from me, Franny?"

"If I'm going to do it, I want you to come up to Carmel with me. Like you used to. I know Mike'll pay your fee like he used to. If he won't, I will."

"Franny, Mike used to hire me to keep you off the booze and the pills and the dope and the . . ."

"Say it, Alex, go ahead and say it. Off the studs. Because I couldn't get enough of a lot of things in those days. Right?!"

"You already said it, kid."

"I'm no kid and I know it! But I still don't want to play this part and the son of a bitch won't let me out. Alex, I'm afraid if I go up there something bad'll happen. So just come with me. A couple of weeks, 'til I settle down."

"Why won't Mike let you out? That doesn't sound like him."

"He says it's for me. That I'll win an Academy Award. Who gives a shit! It'd be for 'supporting actress' anyhow, I'm no goddamn supporting actress."

"You weren't much of a goddamn actress at all when Mike signed you thirty years ago."

"It wasn't thirty!"

"All right, twenty-nine."

"Alex, please, I feel like I'm drowning. Come with me, keep me afloat, Alex please."

"Franny, as the Irish say, 'I'm sorry for your trouble,' but you haven't got real trouble. Other people do. So, I'll tell you what you and I are going to do. You're going to go to Carmel and play the hell out of that part and start a whole new career. And me, I'm going to get into my car, drive away from Larchmont Boulevard and start a whole new career."

I got up from the chair and tossed more than enough money onto the table.

"Alex," she hollered. "You're just like him. A son of a bitch!"

A lot of people turned to look at the son of a bitch who headed past the newsstand and toward the underground parking garage where I had been renting space. My parking spot was paid up to the end of the month, so I figured I'd use it this one more time.

I walked down two flights of stairs once again with the aid of my trusty Malacca. A few years ago on a lark, I had purchased the walking stick during an auction MGM staged to get rid of furniture, wardrobe, props and other memorabilia from their halcyon days when the lion roared. But for almost the last twenty years Leo had lost his voice — and his mane and his pride.

He was King of the Jungle no more. He was a titmouse without any tits. The studio and its assets had been pillaged by a series of buccaneers who didn't give a shit about Gable, Garbo, Tracy, Garson, Garland, Andy Hardy or Boy's Town. They didn't want to make movies. They just wanted to make a quick buck. They stripped the cupboard bare, then sold the wallpaper, the door knobs and the floor boards.

So I got a Malacca cane for eleven dollars. The auctioneer said it had been used by Maurice Chevalier in *Gigi*, but I doubt it. What the hell would Maury be doing with a Malaysian crosier in Paris — even if it was actually the back lot in Culver City?

I walked toward my LeBaron convertible. Mine was the gray one with the handicapped sign in the windshield, parked in a rather dark corner. I was whistling a romantic ballad, "Dancing in the Dark," I believe it was, and pulling the keys out of my pocket when I saw them step out from behind a pillar. First one, then the other. A small man and then a large, very large man.

I recognized the small one, a sleaze named Petey Boyle. The large one I didn't know, nor was I anxious to make his acquaintance. But somehow I had the feeling that it was unavoidable.

"Hello, Night," said Petey Boyle. "Remember me?"

"The odor is familiar."

"Still cracking wise, uh, Night?!"

"Still standing in dark corners, uh, Petey? Who's your friend, Moose Malloy?"

I was sorry I said that. Not because I was afraid it would insult Petey's pal. But because it was an insult to my dear departed friend Mike Mazurki who played the part of Moose in *Murder My Sweet*. I had met Mike at the Cauliflower Club. He was a sweet, intelligent man who had been a lawyer, then a wrestler and then an actor. I went to his funeral over at St. Vladimir's. I knew Mike had a lot more class than this beefy bum, no matter what his name was. But neither of these two lowlifes knew what I was thinking, or talking about.

"He's just a friend," said Petey.

"A hired friend, of course."

"You're for hire, aren't you, Night?"

"Not any more, Petey. Not any more. I'm retired."

"My ex-partner hired you once, remember."

I remembered. Although the whole thing

90

wasn't worth remembering, just another faded file in the folio of an ex-private eye. Neither Petey nor his partner ever got a Boy Scout merit badge, but of the two, his partner was slightly preferable. Besides he was the one who hired me and paid my fee.

"You'll excuse me now, Petey. The air is getting a little close in here and so are you." I started to insert the key.

"You dug up some 'damaging evidence' — cost me my professional reputation, my business."

"Petey, you should've buried the damaging evidence a little deeper and yourself with it."

"You didn't say he was a cripple." The large man spoke in just about the dull, measured tone I would have expected.

"He talks!" I proclaimed.

The large man was not amused. He nodded toward my knees.

"Which is the bad leg?"

The large man kicked me in the shin. He had guessed right. A bolt of pain shot through my left leg and then ricocheted throughout my entire nervous system.

"That one?" He inquired after the fact.

I buckled. Almost dropped. I could hear Petey laughing. The little asshole. I managed to look up. The large man was smiling a scimitar smile and looking at Petey.

I swung the Malacca with all my strength and cracked the large man on the left side of his skull.

The large man dropped unconscious. I knew he would.

After the shockwave, Petey started to move away. But not fast enough. I dropped my keys, grabbed him and slammed him hard against the concrete pillar. With both hands I jammed the length of my cane across his throat and applied pressure. Petey's eyes bulged in agony.

"I'm in a mellow mood, Petey," I said. "So I'm going to dismiss all this. You do the same. Right?"

Petey didn't respond. He couldn't. And I knew it. I applied even more pressure, then eased off.

"Right?"

Petey managed to nod.

"If you don't, the next time I'll pop out your eyeballs — both of them."

I used the cane to help me bend over and pick up the keys. I got into the LeBaron and backed it out, leaving Petey standing there trembling.

The large man was still unconscious.

Farewell, my lovely Larchmont Boule-vard.

Chapter Ten

I drove the LeBaron west on Beverly Boulevard past Doheny where Chasen's used to be. Another culinary casualty. In the old days all the stars used to eat there. Some, like Marilyn Monroe and Yves Montand, even did a little shameless necking while at the time each was married to someone else. But now Chasen's is just a fading memory and the site of Bristol Farms, an upscale market. It could be worse. It could be a McDonald's.

I hung a left on Doheny, south to Burton Way, then west until Burton Way ran into Little Santa Monica. That was the heart of Beverly Hills — if Beverly Hills has a heart.

I parked in the underground public garage on Little Santa Monica and Rodeo Drive.

When I had left my old location on Larchmont I had an empty feeling in the pit of my stomach. But the pain in my leg told me I was doing the smart thing.

I didn't know it then but fate was about to

deal me a new hand, locationwise . . . and otherwise.

I walked past the WRITERS AND ARTISTS BUILDING and headed toward Kramer's Tobacco Shop to see one of my favorite blondes.

When I entered she rushed up to greet me with a kiss. Tina Kramer, the widow Kramer, was in her sixties. The shop had been there since 1952. Tina and her husband Al ran it together until he died in 1973.

Since then she ran it alone, except for some part-time help from diminutive daughter Marsha, who was an actress. Marsha played Wendy in *Peter Pan* with Sandy Duncan on Broadway.

Almost everybody in "the business" who smoked — and some who didn't — stopped in at Kramer's, from Cecil B. DeMille to Henry Wilcoxon, Cary Grant, Yul Brenner, Billy Wilder, Danny Thomas, Danny Kaye, Fred Astaire, Jack Lemmon, Glenn Ford, Hugh O'Brien, Milton Berle, Gene Kelly, James Arness, et cetera.

Groucho Marx used to come in regularly and buy a couple boxes of cheap cigars at a time. He said they were for his gardener. But his gardener didn't smoke.

When I walked in, Mrs. Kramer had been mixing up a blend. She wore a tobacco-

stained smock on which she wiped her to-
bacco-stained hands before she kissed me.
She was a licensed tobacco mixologist —
and an unlicensed philosopher.

I thanked her for the cigarettes she'd sent
while I was mending and told her about my
new vocation.

"Congratulations, Alex. It's about time
you got out of the peeper profession."

"You sound like my mother."

"I'm too young to be your mother. So
you're going to be a writer? Some of my best
customers are writers, you know."

"Yes, I know."

"I've got a few suggestions."

"Shoot," I said.

"Switch from cigarettes to a pipe."

"Why?"

"Writers smoke pipes. Gives them something to do while they're thinking about
plots. Besides, those cigarettes'll do you in."

"Okay," I shrugged. "I'll switch."

"And buy a couple of tweed coats with
suede patches on the elbows."

"Why?"

"That's what real writers wear. Right now
you look like a dick. You dress like a dick.
Besides all your suits have a bulge from that
rod you carry."

"Carried."

"You're still carrying the bulge."

"Anything else?" I lit up a Lucky.

"Yes, rent an office in the WRITERS AND ARTISTS BUILDING on the corner."

"Why?"

"Billy Wilder, Ray Bradbury, Michael Blankfort and a lot of other great writers worked there. Some of it might rub off on you."

"Osmosis."

"Mossis, schmosis. Besides the rent is reasonable. The owner has a thing about writers. There's a waiting list but I've got connections."

"Anything else?"

"Yes. Get rid of that cane and those dark glasses. You look like a blind man. Whoever heard of a blind writer?"

"Homer was blind."

"Homer who?"

"Never mind. Pretty soon I won't need the cane. But the glasses cost two hundred bucks."

"They saw you coming. Put 'em in your pocket."

She reached up, took the Lucky out of my mouth and snuffed it in an ashtray.

"I'll mix you a nice blend of tobacco. We'll pick out a couple of pipes I've got on sale, then I'll call Henry Fenenbock, Jr."

I put the sunglasses in my pocket. I had a feeling she might reach up and grab them too.

"Who's Henry Fenenbock, Jr.?"

"He owns the corner building. You're in luck, a writer up there just croaked — a non-smoker, they haven't even moved his junk out yet." Mrs. Kramer was moving toward the tobacco mixing counter.

"Did he croak up there?" I asked.

"What difference does it make?"

"None to him, I guess." I lit another Lucky. "Come to think of it, so was Milton."

"So was Milton what?"

"Blind."

Chapter Eleven

I stood at the entrance hallway of the WRITERS AND ARTISTS BUILDING studying the plaque attached to the wall:

Henry Fenenbock, a friend
to all writers and artists
From his tenants

While I appreciated most of Mrs. Kramer's advice, I knew she was a little out of touch with what writers and everybody else in town were wearing. Most of the males and females in "the business" that I came across, clients and culprits, looked like mannequins from Banana Republic. Wrinkled chic, unstructured *haute monde*. And usually unisex — at least until you put it on — or took it off.

And while there's something to be said for being *au courant*, there's also something to be said for not looking squirrelly. So I compromised. Corduroy pants from Sears and a tweed sport coat (with suede patch elbows) from Pendleton. No sunglasses, but I still carried the cane.

From the plaque, my gaze shifted to the building directory and spotted my name. It had recently been added to the list of writer and artist tenants.

I smiled.

Then I glanced outside to see if any of the passersby took notice of the new writer on the block.

There was a beige Bentley double-parked at the curb. The chauffeur was at the open rear door. An impeccably haberdashed, immaculately groomed, imperiously mannered gentleman alighted from the vehicle and approached the entrance. As he entered, the gentleman deigned a priggish look of evaluation in my direction. He carried an ebony walking stick with what appeared to be a wad of gold at the top. He reminded me of Clifton Webb in *Laura*.

"Good morning," I smiled.

"Is it?"

"Well, it's a good day to be alive."

"Yes."

"You have an office here?"

"A suite," he corrected. "The only suite."

With his ebony walking stick he pointed to his name on the directory. E. Elliott Elliot.

"E. Elliott Elliot," I said with instant recognition. "Say, didn't you win an Academy Award once?"

"Twice."

"Excuse me," I cleared my throat.

"You are excused, by the by." With his ebony walking stick he pointed to my Malacca cane. "Is that a necessity, or an affectation?"

"A temporary necessity," I smiled again, then pointed my Malacca cane to his ebony waking stick. "And you?"

"Touché, dear boy — and good day." E. Elliott Elliot proceeded in his imperious way up the flight of stairs.

As I "caned" my way up to my new office I recollected what I'd learned from Mrs. Kramer about the WRITERS AND ARTISTS BUILDING and what I'd gleaned from simple observation.

This three-story structure on the northwest corner of Little Santa Monica and Rodeo Drive houses several shops and boutiques on the ground floor. Each of the upper two floors consists of a wide, but moody center hallway flanked by warren-like twelve- by fourteen-foot offices. No central air conditioning. No hot water. No elevator.

It was built in 1920 and changed hands several times until Henry Fenenbock, who made a fortune painting turtles at the Chicago World's Fair, bought it in 1958. The original Fenenbock died in 1981. His son, Henry Jr. maintains an office — number 205 — in the center of the second floor but is seldom, if ever, seen by his tenants, or by anybody else.

On the door of office 205 there are a couple of phone numbers. A voice on an answering machine says, "Please leave a message." If you're lucky, in a few days a lady will return the call and politely tell you there is no vacancy but there is a long waiting list — not months, years.

I never did find out how Mrs. Kramer managed to leapfrog the list.

I stood in the center of the room surveying my newly acquired realm, puffing on my newly acquired pipe. "Cheapers" had already transferred the Larchmont stuff I needed.

I had tossed my new elbow patch sport coat across a Naugahyde couch. Other appointments included my old roll-top desk and chair, a left-behind straight-back chair, a newly installed telephone and a non-electric Royal typewriter.

Plus a dictionary, a thesaurus, a hot plate, a dented aluminum coffee pot, a couple of restaurant coffee cups and spoons, a ream of unlined white paper, two more pipes, a half pound can of Mrs. Kramer's mixture tobacco and a box of kitchen matches.

It didn't take long to settle in. Now all I had to do was settle in on what I was going to write. I moved toward the window and looked out. The writer who croaked had a corner office overlooking Rodeo Drive. I had a direct, unobstructed view of what used to be Carroll and Co., one of the oldest and best known men's clothing shops in Beverly Hills.

Only it wasn't there any more.

For years the heads of wardrobe departments from motion picture and television studios sent their wardrobe people there to fit the stars of their features and series. The inside of the place looked like a shop in England. And so did the cut of their suits and sport coats.

It was not uncommon to see Cary Grant, Fred Astaire and Gene Kelly there at the same time, along with other well-dressed actors, writers, producers and directors. In those days when an actor like Dick Crenna came in and spent a thousand dollars at a crack he was considered a high roller. Today a Chester Barrie suit off the rack goes for two thousand dollars. One suit — with one pair of pants and no vest.

I was a regular customer. Twice a year. That's because twice a year Dick Carroll and his son John staged a very screwy semi-annual sale — the mother of all sales in Beverly Hills — more like a jousting contest.

At nine-twenty-nine on a Saturday morning in July and January there were approximately five hundred people at the main entrance on Rodeo Drive. There were approximately five hundred more people at the side entrance on Little Santa Monica Blvd. These citizens — mature, marginally sophisticated people — actors, writers, producers, directors stood jammed shoulder to shoulder next to lawyers, stock brokers, agents and assorted types whose annual median income easily exceeded two hundred and fifty thousand American. They mashed and ground against each other, some attended by wives and sweethearts, until the stroke of nine-thirty when both doors burst open.

At that time the five hundred knights at the front charged through the main entrance and stampeded in an easterly direction, while the five hundred knaves at the side entrance charged through and swarmed toward the west. In a scene out of Cecil B. DeMille's *The Crusades* the two armies clashed somewhere in between and the battle was joined. Sudden enemies tore each other to tatters while everybody grabbed seven or eight suits, a half dozen sport coats, assorted sweaters and several shirts in his size, knowing full well that he was going to purchase only one, maybe two, of each item and discard the rest on the wrong rack or on the floor.

Aslant, six in a row, the bargain seekers stood, swayed, squatted and squeezed in front of a single looking glass while slipping a sport coat over one shoulder and a suit over the other, trying to ascertain simultaneously the sartorial effect of their potential purchase.

The combat and confusion continued amid bloodied noses, battered ribs and grievous aggression. The women were the worst offenders, wielding handbags and hangers with reckless abandon and malicious intent while providing pasturage and passage for their wards.

I am not embarrassed to admit my semi-annual participation in those proceedings for the past fifteen or more years. Why should I be? Several years ago I spotted Lew Wasserman, the head of MCA among the aggressors. Mr. Wasserman never wore a dunce cap in school. Brains was his Sunday suit and he wore it everyday.

Looking down from my office now, instead of Carroll and Co. there was a brand new structure with a brand new sign — TOMMY HILFIGER — a more casual and less elegant clothing store, another sign of the times.

In August of 1996, Carroll and Co. moved a couple of blocks east to 425 Canon Drive in a building combining the best of the old traditions with a lighter, brighter atmosphere. The current customers include Tom Cruise, Robin Williams, Robert Redford and Harrison Ford. But the clothes have the same labels — Hickey-Freeman, Oxxford, Chester Barrie of Saville Row — and at the same precious price tags. Well, what the hell, class costs — at least when it comes to clothes.

So, the bad news was that Carroll and Co. moved. The good news, the semi-annual sales still go on.

Meanwhile, even though Carroll and Co. had moved, I was lucky. I could still enjoy the view of one of the most elite streets in Beverly Hills — or the world.

— Maybe not so lucky. A view can be distracting to a writer. So can a lot of other things — as I found out.

"Mr. Night?"

A. Night had been painted on the wooden nameplate, a nameplate like all the other nameplates on all the other doors.

The door was open and she stood by the nameplate.

"Mr. Night?" she repeated.

I just might have acquired a new favorite blonde. She was beautiful, with lips that looked like they had just licked something sweet — and fresh as a spring garden. I weighed her in at 126 pounds. Blue eyes that didn't have, or need, makeup. Short honey-blonde hair. Slender but strong hands. A clean, clear California complexion. Long, lovely legs. She wore a dark blue skirt and jersey blouse that matched her eyes.

"Ye . . . yes," I stammered.

"I'm G. Rose across the hall. May I use your phone? Local call."

"Miz Rose, you may use anything I have."

"Thanks. Just the phone. I don't have one in my office. Too distracting."

I stood there mumchance while she walked to the phone and punched a number. She walked even better than she stood still. And that jersey blouse pendulated just right.

She smiled at me as she listened to a recorded message, then spoke into the phone.

"Sorry, Duke, can't make lunch today. Right in the middle of a murder." She hung up and tapped the phone twice.

"Who done it?" I said cleverly.

"That's what I've got to figure out this afternoon."

"Good luck."

"Luck hasn't got a damn thing to do with it. By three o'clock I'll narrow the murder down to four suspects on page 223. By noon tomorrow on page 308, those six immortal letters T-H-E-E-N-D."

"That's it?"

"That's it."

"How long have you been working on it?"

"Same as all the others. Eleven days."

To borrow a phrase from Dashiell Hammett, she made it sound as easy as eating gravy.

"You write a novel . . . an entire novel . . . in just eleven days?"

"Exactly. Twenty eight pages a day. Totals 308 pages per novel."

"Simple as slicing salami," I said, thinking I was improving a little on Dash.

"Not quite," she admitted.

"And they all get published?"

"That's the idea."

"Have I ever read any of your books?"

"Maybe."

I riffled through the tables of my memory. There were a lot of female mystery writers lately, Julie Smith, Sara Paretesky, Sue Grafton, Linda Barnes, Patricia Cornwell . . .

"G. Rose," I said aloud and repeated, "G. Rose . . ."

"No. No . . ."

She walked out of the door and for a moment I thought that that was the end of the conversation, but she beckoned from the hallway.

"Step across into the Twilight Zone," she invited.

With no hesitation and great anticipation I followed her through the hallway and into the opposite office.

The room was the same size as mine, but appeared larger because of the furnishings, or lack of furnishings.

Spartan. Strictly utilitarian. A computer-type table, a word processor, two straight-back chairs.

Not even a coat rack, just a screw-in hook behind the door. No phone.

On the floor two tall stacks of books, hardcovers and paperbacks by several different authors.

She let me just stand there a moment for the full effect. It was effective. Then she pointed to the books.

"That's me. John Grim, Bart Cord, Gray Lugar, Russ Spiker, et cetera, et cetera, et cetera."

You could have knocked me over with a jersey blouse.

"I have read you. You're tough."

"At these prices, tough comes easy. Especially when the payoff includes television and an occasional low budget movie. What do you write, Mr. Night?"

The truth was that about the only thing I had ever written was bills to my clients, plus some stuff for a short story course I took at UCLA, so I thought I'd play it cute.

"I'm still a virgin."

She let it pass.

"You can call me Alex."

"Okay. Is Night your real name?"

"Nyktas. In Greek it means . . ."

"Night."

"Right. How'd you know?"

"My real name is Triandafelos. In Greek it means . . ."

"Rose. Yes, Santa Claus, there is a Virginia."

"How's that?"

"Never mind."

"Well," she smiled. "We do have something in common."

"Not too much." I gave her the up and down. "I'm happy to say."

"Yes." She looked at me, then at the door. "Well . . ."

"I know, page 223. Uh, any time you want to use the phone . . . or anything else . . ."

"I know."

"I meant a dictionary . . . thesaurus . . ."

"Thanks, I have one of each at home."

"You write at home too?"

"Not mysteries."

"What?"

"My doctoral thesis."

"Oh, on what?"

"It's called, 'The Crime of Punishment.' "

"You're deeper than you are tall. How long have you been working on that?"

"Two years."

I would have liked to linger a while longer. What I would have really liked was to seduce her, or have her seduce me. But as Scarlett O'Hara remarked in the last reel, "Tomorrow is another day." And this was not the last reel. I felt it in my bones.

I walked to the door, doing my best imitation of John Wayne making an exit, paused by the nameplate, turned and gave the woman I loved my million-dollar smile.

"If you do need anything, just whistle. I'll be right across the hall. By the way, what's the 'G.' stand for?"

"Goldie." She pointed to the processor. "But right now, I'm 'Trig Barker.' "

"Yeah, well, Happy Ending, Trig."

Chapter Twelve

Some time went by. Looking back now, I'm not exactly sure just how much time, but on my roll-top desk at the office there was a title sheet on top of 308 pages.

Pipe smoke curled across the title sheet as I sat there studying the words that I had written on that first page:

THE BIG CHANGEOVER
a novel by
A. NIGHT

I lifted the top sheet and was satisfied with what I had written on it.

The only trouble was — the rest of the 308 pages were blank.

And so was I.

For hours, days, weeks, months, years, for all the time in all the calendars in all the world I had sat at the desk or gazed out of the window, or walked around the block, or watched E. Elliott Elliot come and go in his beige Bentley, or most of all thought about

G. Rose in her office across the hall.

I could sum her up in four words. Spec. Tac. U. Lar.

In actual fact it hadn't really been that long. She had probably written only two or three novels while I worked on my title. But for all I knew she might even have finished her doctorate.

I'd always leave the door open hoping she'd come in and seduce me — or even use the phone. But she never called Duke again, or anybody else. G. Rose just kept knocking off her 28 pages a day as if that big, good looking guy across the hall didn't exist.

She wasn't in the Twilight Zone, I was.

The truth is I don't know how anybody ever got any work done in Beverly Hills. Everything about the 5.5 square miles of the city conspires to distract a serious writer like myself from pursuing his profession. It's just so damn divagating and beautiful — from the elegant ladies who pound for pound are the most maddeningly gorgeous and expensively groomed women on earth, to the architecture and automobiles that make you pause and ponder the wonders of the capitalist world. The Union of the Soviet Socialist Republics didn't stand the chance of a wax dummy in hell.

The city was incorporated in 1914 with a

population of 550. Today there are 33,000 people and 33,000 trees planted there. Another 7,000 people like me drive in to work everyday. I hope they get more done in their daily endeavors than I have. The yearly household income after taxes is $137,178. Somebody's got my share.

Besides walking around the streets searching for inspiration, I took to strolling through Beverly Gardens right across the way from the WRITERS AND ARTISTS BUILDING among the joggers and picnickers. Fourteen blocks of trees, shrubs and flowers along Santa Monica Boulevard. I fancied myself as Henry David Thoreau on Walden Pond nearer to God. It didn't work.

I might have been better off on Devil's Island where things weren't so damn pleasant. Where the hell were those millions of stories with their tongues hanging out waiting to be told? I couldn't make sense out of a single one.

Besides G. Rose and E. Elliott Elliot, I made the acquaintance of several of the other writers in the building. Wes Weston, a Texan about seven feet tall who dressed and talked like Randolph Scott, was among the more memorable. A number of decades ago Wes created a western series — in this case "created" involved changing the title and character names of a John Wayne picture called *Red River* to *Cattle Drive*. They made over 150 episodes and Wes made a fortune. He's made nothing since then, but he buttonholes everybody and talks about how westerns will be back and so will he. Meanwhile, you can see *Cattle Drive* on Saturday afternoons on cable and Wes Weston on weekdays at the WRITERS AND ARTISTS BUILDING.

Morgan Noble was another tenant. Morgan is a woman. Although sometimes it was hard to tell. Her hair was bobbed and so was her bosom. She dressed in men's clothes and politically was a direct descendant of Ayn Rand. She wrote novels that were to the right of Czar Nicholas. But she wrote them dirty so they sold reasonably well. She and E. Elliott Elliot went out of their way to insult each other.

He called her Madame Ovary.

She said the E. in his name stood for Effete.

Then there were the Bernstein brothers, Bruce and Bernie, a set of five-foot-five twins who not only wrote together but finished each other's sentences in casual conversation.

"Hello there . . ." Brother Bruce.

". . . how are you?" Brother Bernie.

"We're going out . . ." Brother Bruce.

". . . to have lunch." Brother Bernie.

"Care to join us . . ." Brother Bruce.

". . . for a bite?" Brother Bernie.

"No, thanks. Not today." Alex Night.

Meanwhile, every time I started to write I kept getting interrupted. Like Dick Powell in the best picture that was ever made about Hollywood, *The Bad and the Beautiful*. He played James Lee Bartlow, a writer from the South who was brought here to work on a screenplay for Kirk Douglas, who played a producer named Jonathon Shields.

Whenever Powell started to type, his wife Gloria Grahame would sashay into the room, flutter her Southern Belle eyelashes and other parts and distract him from the assignment. Grahame got an Academy Award.

But I wasn't distracted by anybody who looked like Gloria Grahame. It was either Myron Garter on the phone or, more often, my mother wanting to know when she could tell her friends that my novel was at the bookstore and to make sure that I dedicated it to her.

Once again I decided to give it another shot. Like Dick Powell I started to write . . .

I got as far as "It started out strictly routine . . ."

The phone rang. I picked up the receiver.

"Hello, Mom."

"Mom? Is this Alex Night?"

I recognized the voice, Cynthia Alderdyce.

"Yes, Mrs. A."

"Alex, how are you feeling?"

"First rate. How's everything in the desert?"

"Don't know. I'm back in Beverly Hills."

"When did you get back?"

"A few days ago. Why didn't you tell me you changed your phone number?"

"I haven't told anybody. I've changed a lot of things, including my profession."

"Is that so?"

"I'm a writer now."

"We'll see about that."

"Thanks." I looked at my typewriter. "Well, I appreciate your calling, Mrs. A., I'll . . ."

"Alex, I want you to come over to the house, three o'clock this afternoon. Don't be late."

"Mrs. A., I'm busy . . ."

"Not too busy for this. It's important. Be here."

"Yes, Ma'am."

"Are you going to make more money as a writer?"

"I don't know. But money can't buy happiness."

"Money is happiness," she said. "Three o'clock."

I hung up the phone and looked at the typewriter. So much for *The Big Changeover*. I had just enough time to grab some lunch and hie toward the *hoi-polloi*.

My old pal Lieutenant Garter had recommended me to Mrs. Alderdyce about four years ago. The case had to do with one of her son Colin's three divorces. As I said, ordinarily I didn't take divorce jobs. But Mrs. Alderdyce had made me an extra ordinary offer.

I'd been working for her on and off ever since.

I had no idea what she had in mind this time. There was only one way to find out. But if it had anything to do with detective work, I'd have to say no. I was a writer now.

I put on my coat, picked up my cane, patted the typewriter and went out the door.

As I stepped into the hallway and closed the door to my office, I glanced, as had become my usual habit, at G. Rose's door just across the way. Usually — as a matter of fact, invariably — that door was closed.

Not this time. This time it was ajar. And

this time G. Rose was standing there almost as if she had been waiting for me. At least that's what I wanted to think.

"Hello, Trig," said I.

"John Grim, at the moment."

"Glad to meet you, Mr. Grim."

"Mind if I ask you a personal question?"

"The more personal the better."

"Why did you quit being a private eye?"

"Are you doing research for a book, Mr. Grim?"

"No, just curious."

"Who told you that I was a private eye?"

"Your greatest admirer showed me the Palm Springs story she clipped out of the L.A. *Times*."

"My mother? Or Mrs. Kramer?"

"Mrs. Kramer."

"You smoke?"

"Not anymore, but I stop in to pick up mints."

"You ever stop someplace to have lunch or dinner?"

"Occasionally."

"Occasionally with somebody? Maybe somebody who used to be a private eye — and would be happy to answer all of your personal questions?"

"Maybe. Ask me when I'm done with *Lady Like a Whore*."

"When will that be, Mr. Grim?"

"Tomorrow."

"I cannot tell you with what anticipation I look forward to that morrow."

There was the faint fragrance of some perfume and I thought I detected just a trace of mint. I noticed that she wore plain golden earrings and a soft cotton turtleneck sweater, blue, that swelled amply in each of the right places. I stepped a step closer to her.

"What are you doing?"

"Nothing. I just wanted to feel your presence . . ."

"My what?" She smiled. "Back."

"I'm backing." I put it in reverse just a bit. "Those are lovely earrings."

"The earrings are higher."

So they were.

"Goldie, do you know what I'm going to do right now?"

"What?"

"I'm going to stop by and give Mrs. Kramer a kiss." I bowed a sort of Errol Flynn bow, touching my invisible breastplate with my cane as if it were the flat of a sword, then turned toward the stairway.

"Oh, Alex," she called.

"Yes?"

"I'll tell you something else."

"What?"

"About your being a private eye — Elliott told me too," she smiled.

"Yes . . . well . . . I'll give Mrs. Kramer two kisses."

Chapter Thirteen

I grabbed a sandwich with both hands, gobbled it up and washed it down with a large Coke. I did stop by Mrs. Kramer's A) to deliver the two kisses, B) to find out what she knew about Goldie Rose that I ought to know before I took her to dinner, C) to pick up some Luckies.

I succeeded in accomplishing neither A nor B because there were too many customers in the shop. So I settled for C and headed for the LeBaron. Cynthia Alderdyce lived on Ambassador Drive.

I drove north on Rodeo Drive into the residential district of Beverly Hills. Most of the residential streets in that area are lined with tall wind-bent palm trees, streets like Beverly, Canon, Crescent, and Rexford. But not Rodeo Drive. I don't like palm trees, at least not around houses where people live. To me palm trees look like elongated telephone poles with clumps of green bird shit on top.

Rodeo drive has real trees, like in the

Midwest, birch I think they are, or maybe elm. But they look like trees, not wooden mutants.

I flipped on the radio and the Andrews Sisters were singing "I Can Dream, Can't I?" I was daydreaming about what it would be like to settle into a long warm night with Goldie Rose as I made the four-way stops at Carmelita, Elevado, Lomitas and finally Sunset Boulevard.

On Sunset I cut up Benedict Canyon parallel to the west side of The Beverly Hills Hotel. In the past I had met many clients there for breakfast, lunch or dinner while they told me about the adverse circumstances which impelled them to require my confidential services.

Nine out of ten of those clients wasted a lot of my time trying to convince me that they were innocent victims of fragile fate. That they had actually meant well, but somehow stumbled over their good intentions and ended up having their pictures taken in bed with their best friend's wife or husband. After the first decade damn few people could tell me a tale I hadn't already heard.

But I was neither judge nor jury. I just collected my fee and did what I could to get them out of a jam. In many cases I was successful, and they swore they had seen the light. But you'd be surprised — or maybe you wouldn't — at the rate of recidivism among my clients. About sixty-five percent were repeaters. But that was in another life. I was a writer now.

On Benedict I passed Lexington, then Chevy Chase — the street, not the actor — and Summit Drive. To the right was Pickfair, the fabled estate built and lived in by Mary Pickford, America's Sweetheart, and Douglas Fairbanks, America's Swash-buckler — until they ceased being sweet-hearts and got a divorce. She got the estate and he got the buckle.

On one side of the next intersection was Tower Road where John Barrymore in his mansion drank himself to death trying to ward off demons that only he could see. And at the crest of Tower Road Valentino had built his Eagle's Nest.

On the other side of the intersection was Ambassador Drive. I took a left.

Ambassador Drive was about as exclusive as it gets. Another grand lady, Loretta Young, had been a neighbor of Cynthia Alderdyce for a long time. I had seen Loretta Young at a couple of charity affairs just before the end. She had looked as at-tractive, make that beautiful, as she did in

Call of the Wild, *Farmer's Daughter* and *Key to the City*.

I got as close to her as I could and looked for tell-tale marks of plastic surgery. If they were there, they told no tale.

Why was it that most of the beautiful women were born before my time? Loretta Young, Cynthia Alderdyce, Gene Tierny, Hedy Lamarr, Vivian Leigh — most, but not all. There was Goldie Rose. We were contemporaries. And I hoped companions.

I pulled into the circular driveway off Ambassador Drive. I got out of the LeBaron, cane in hand, walked to the front door and pushed the chime button with the tip of my Malacca.

As usual, Peter the butler responded. He looked and spoke like a character actor from the early talkies. I liked him. He always treated me civilly.

Peter knew that I was there at this time because Mrs. Alderdyce told me to be there at this time. He extracted his pocket watch and checked the hour. I thought it was very civil of him not to chastise me for being three minutes late.

I looked around the center hall of the mansion. Nothing had changed since the last time I had been there. The place was still a glittering monument to extravagance.

I followed Peter at a respectable distance as he led me through Versailles Palace to the patio.

The patio was in keeping with the rest of the shameless structure.

Mrs. Alderdyce sat at one of the pink patio tables. Across from her sat a man. In front of each of them sat a glass. Hers, I knew, held bourbon; his looked like lemonade, pink lemonade. Also in front of him lay a folder, legal size, with papers inside. Next to that, a slim, expensive, leather briefcase.

The man rose as Peter and I approached. He looked like a combination of Willard Scott and Ed MacMahon. The sort of fellow whose picture was probably on his stationery. His demeanor did not disguise the fact that he would have preferred to be someplace else. But he smiled at me and then looked at Mrs. Alderdyce to make sure she saw that he was being nice to me.

"Alex," she said. "Thank you for coming." As if I had much choice.

I nodded politely.

"Alex, this is Bernard Wentworth."

Bernard Wentworth extended a bloodless hand. It was like touching a frog's belly. We shook.

"He's with AmBrit Insurance. He has

something for you. Don't you, Mr. Wentworth?"

Wentworth nodded pleasurelessly and proceeded to open the folder.

"Would you care for a drink, Alex?" Mrs. A. inquired.

"No thanks."

At that, Peter vanished.

In the acre or so of backyard there was a tennis court and a massive swimming pool with an inflated, floating, white rubber swan.

Colin Alderdyce was on the diving board on the far end of the pool. He waved at me. I waved back. Then Colin executed a perfect dive. Almost halfway across the pool he surfaced and swam toward us.

But my attention was elsewhere.

My attention was on the Valkyrie who stood alongside of the pool. Only a string bikini stood between her and nakedness.

In the sunlight, her skin-toned bikini was almost invisible. Almost. And she stood there shimmering in that sunlight — all six feet of her. There should have been a law against her.

Valkyrie watched as Colin surfaced, then she undulated along the pool as he swam. Who said that monuments can't move?

My trance was broken by the sound of

Bernard Wentworth's voice.

"If you'll just sign here, Mr. Night." He had placed a legal-size form on the table near where I was standing.

"What for?" I inquired.

"For ten thousand dollars," Mrs. Alderdyce responded.

The last time somebody had given me ten thousand dollars was never.

"A small token," Mrs. A. continued, "of AmBrit's gratitude for the recovery of my jewelry and for that."

She pointed to my left leg.

I was pleasantly shocked. As a matter of fact it took all my will power to keep from jumping up like one of those guys in a Toyota commercial.

"If you expect a protest," I finally said, "you're going to be disappointed."

Bernard Wentworth handed me a Mont Blanc pen. I signed the form at the place he had marked with an X.

"It's the least AmBrit can do," said Mrs. A. to Mr. W. "Isn't it, Mr. Wentworth?"

Wentworth sighed, nodded and handed me the check.

By now Colin had emerged from the pool and was approaching. The Valkyrie picked up a pink towel about the size of a baby blanket and began to dry him off. As she did her body shimmered even more. Particularly her upper bodies.

All the best Japanese and German designers in the world could not have improved on that chassis. Seamless. Every curve, arch, sweep and bend.

Like a fool Colin took the towel with a smile and continued drying as he moved closer — the Valkyrie at his side.

"How's the hero?" Colin smiled at me.

"Flush." I put the check in my pocket and patted it reverently.

"You deserve it and more," Colin said.

I was gazing at his statuesque sidekick but that wasn't what he meant, I'm sure. I guess Mrs. A. noticed my gaze.

"Alex," Mrs. Alderdyce said, "this is last year's Miss Sweden and this month's centerfold. Now everybody go away. I want to talk to Alex alone."

Bernard Wentworth zipped up his slim, expensive, leather briefcase.

"Pleasure doing business with AmBrit," I said to Mr. Wentworth. "And nice visiting with you, Miss Sweden."

"Ingrid," she said without trace of an accent.

"Well, congratulations, Alex," Colin smiled.

"You too, Colin," I replied, trying not to look at Ingrid.

When the others dispersed, Cynthia Alderdyce rose and looked out toward the inflated white swan floating in the pool.

"How about a little stroll, Alex?"

"Sure," I said. "Good for the gam."

We walked along the deck in silence, Cynthia Alderdyce, me, and my cane, until I felt I ought to say something.

"Thanks," I patted the check again. "I know it wasn't AmBrit's idea."

"Over the past forty years I've given them a lot of business. So don't even mention it."

Silence for a few more steps.

"But," she said, "there is a slight *'quid pro quo.'* "

"Mention it."

"The man who was killed."

"Bogus number two?"

"Yes. In a way I feel responsible."

"Why? I'm the one who put the slugs into him."

"But who threw him off the roof?"

"Don't know. Don't care. Neither should you."

I didn't want to admit to her, or to myself, that I had been thinking about that and about Bogus number one. But that was ancient history. Over and done with. I was a writer now, I kept telling myself.

"Alex, I'm not asking you to find the killer, but . . ."

"But?"

"Well, I'd just like to know something about him, I mean the man who was killed."

"Why? What?"

"Well, did he have . . . what do they call it — 'priors'?"

"That's what they call it."

"A wife? Children, you know . . ."

"Yeah, I know." I smiled at the spicy tomato. "You're not so tough."

"Yes I am. Tougher than you think. There's nothing I'm afraid of . . . except . . ." She stopped walking.

"Except?"

She pointed to the pool with the floating swan. The water was calm now, except for a few ripples around the swan.

"That." She stared at the pool. "Never could learn to swim. Dream about drowning. Wake up in a sweat. I'd have the damn thing filled in if it weren't for . . ."

"Colin?"

"He loves to swim," she nodded.

"Colin is old enough to get a pool of his own."

"Don't be nasty."

I knew I had hurt her. I suppose I shouldn't have said it. But I thought of a song Connie Francis used to sing. "Everybody is somebody's fool," the lyrics went, "there's no exception to the rule." Well, Mrs. A. was a fool when it came to her son. It was hard to believe he was her son, hers and the wildcatter's. How two tough, independent people could have bred such a bland, self-serving sponger was a genealogical bafflement. At least it was to me.

I didn't know all the details but I'd heard that she had backed him more than once, and heavily, in schemes that went bust. That wouldn't have been so bad — his old man went bust a few times too — but with his own money and his own sweat. Each time it happened to Colin he was off playing tennis or on another honeymoon.

Still, I was sorry I said it. And sorrier that I hurt her.

"Okay, Mrs. A., I'll find out what I can."

"Thanks. And Alex, whatever you do find out, report directly to me. As always."

She reached up with both hands and kissed me on the cheek.

"You're not so tough either," she said.

Chapter Fourteen

I couldn't refuse Cynthia Alderdyce. For a lot of reasons. There was that ten-thousand-dollar check which I had already deposited before the bank closed. But there was more than that.

I would have done it, check or no check. She was a rarity. The kind of woman who was concerned about the family of someone who meant to do her harm.

The kind of woman who went out of her way to help somebody who needed help, and that help — that had included me more than once.

The kind of woman who, in spite of all her money and mansions, had been dealt some bad breaks. The worst was losing the one man that she'd ever loved. Then there was Colin.

With all the parties, all the people around her, all the places she could go, Cynthia Alderdyce was alone in the world.

It was the least I could do for her. Besides it wasn't as if she'd asked me to solve the murder. That was somebody else's concern. All I had to do was a little checking around on somebody who was already dead.

There was no risk. And it wouldn't be all that complicated or time consuming.

Actually it was pretty simple. Not as if I was going back into the detective business again.

Subtle schemer that I am, I was going to let my friend Myron Garter do most of the leg work while I tried to whistle up a plot for *The Big Changeover* and charm the pants off Goldie Rose.

I steered the LeBaron toward the recently renovated Civic Center complex on Rexford Drive between Santa Monica and Burton Way. The Spanish Baroque architecture, dominated by the old stately tower, houses the Beverly Hills City Hall, Public Library, the new Fire and Police Departments.

Since I didn't want to see the Mayor, read a book or report a fire, that left the Police Department.

The old Police Headquarters was as cluttered as a Hong Kong harbor. The new joint is about four times the size of the old and contains offices for all administrative and field operations, secured detention areas, a state of the art jail facility and a computer-automated firing range for weapons training.

I drove through the Shangri La–like setting, parked in the handicapped zone and walked across to the entrance, which is on the second floor. On the wall of the reception room there are pictures of all the Beverly Hills Police Chiefs — from the first, Charles C. Blair to the incumbent, Marvin D. Iannone. There have been only seven. It's a pretty steady job.

But the largest photograph in the room includes Edward G. Robinson, who became famous in the title role of *Little Caesar*, standing with Chief Blair and two other officers. Robinson is wearing a loud check sport coat and holding a cigar in his left hand. The picture is inscribed:

To C. C. Blair
what a quartet
All the best
Edward G. Robinson

I knew officer Paul Medina who was on duty and on the telephone. I motioned to the stairway. He nodded and kept on talking, his dialogue liberally sprinkled with "yes, Ma'am"s. Cane in hand, I proceeded up the stairs.

The Beverly Hills Police Department has a force of 132 sworn officers — "sworn" means they carry guns. The guns they carry are Sig Sauer Semi Automatics, the Rolls Royces of weaponry. They have a choice of either 9 mm with a thirteen round clip plus one in the chamber, or a .45 with a seven round clip and one in the hole. Garter carried the .45.

There's also a support staff of sixty who don't carry. These include Parking Enforcement, Traffic Control, Communications, Jailers — often referred to as "hosts" — and the clerical staff, two of whom are lovely ladies I've known for a long time. One of them announced me to Myron, pressed the release buzzer and I walked through the blue door.

The detectives' cubicles are located on the span that bridges across Rexford connecting the Police Department to City Hall. They've got the best view of all the city employees.

Garter's cubicle is smack in the center of the span. His detail is "Robbery — Homicide." Since there was only one homicide in Beverly Hills last year, most of his work has to do with robbery.

Garter was gnawing on a Baby Ruth bar and assuring some taxpayer that the Beverly

Hills Police Department was on the case and that results would be forthcoming soon. I waited.

When Garter finished, he swiveled in my direction and smiled.

"Myron," I said, "you solve all your cases on the seat of your pants?"

"Sit down, shamus, and take a load off your cane."

I declined his invitation, saying I knew how busy he was and didn't want to be a burden. After the requisite bantering I got around to Mrs. Alderdyce and her request concerning Bogus number one, his family and heirs. Would Myron do a little digging, unofficially of course? He put up a mild protest as I knew he would, but agreed to find out what he could, as I knew he would — after extracting a promise from me to buy him a first-class dinner that night at a restaurant of his choice. The ten grand made that a cinch.

Then he got a phone call on his direct line and his mood changed perceptibly. When I heard him say, "Rhoda, I told you not to call, we've got nothing to talk about . . ." I took it as my cue to get the hell out. For a couple of people who had nothing to talk about, they were going at it hot and heavy when I walked away.

I retraced my steps to the LeBaron, drove to my usual parking spot and headed for the WRITERS AND ARTISTS BUILDING to resume my literary career.

Walking back to the office I spotted the beige Bentley double-parked right in front of the building.

I met E. Elliott Elliot and his walking stick as he was descending the stairway from his suite. He didn't exactly look like he had put in a hard day at the office. He was a walking testament to Saville Row. He wore a gray double-breasted suit with a faint plaid pattern that looked like it had never been sat in. His face was as fresh and as smooth as if he had just stepped out of a barber shop. Matter of fact I detected an aroma of lilac.

"How do you do, Mr. Elliot."

"I do splendidly, and you may omit the mister."

"Thank you."

Then he startled me.

"Would you care to join me for dinner tonight?"

"Thanks, but I've already got a date."

"With Miss Rose?"

"Not tonight." He wasn't shy about asking questions, I thought to myself.

"Well perhaps some other time." Elliot motioned his stick toward my leg. "How is the recovery coming along?"

"It's coming."

"Do you, like Mark McPherson, have a silver shinbone as a result of your encounter with the lawless element?"

"Mark? . . . Oh . . ." I remembered in the movie *Laura*; Dana Andrews played a detective named Mark McPherson who got shot in the leg and had a silver bone grafted in to replace his original.

"No. This lawless element missed the bone. Just tore up some cartilage."

"You must have had many adventures as a private investigator."

"Not too many."

"You must tell me all about it sometime. I'm fascinated by danger. Other people's. Well ta-ta."

He left taking the faint aroma of lilac with him. I watched as his chauffeur opened the rear door of the Bentley, then I entered the building as the car pulled away.

Most of the offices in the building were closed. Tonight there was just the occasional clackety-clack of a typewriter echoing in the hall, but then just about all of the writers had converted to word processors.

I recalled the story about Harry Cohn, the tyrannical boss of Columbia, who decreed that all of the writers on his lot would come in at nine and stay until six, with an hour for lunch. Since Cohn was paying for a full day's work, he wanted to hear typewriters clackety-clacking from the writers' building all day long.

In the summer he'd skulk outside the open windows and listen. Writers would alternately stand guard, watching for his approach. When he was spotted coming, every typewriter in the building began to clatter.

After a while Cohn caught on.

"Goddam liars!" he screamed one day.

I looked for a white line of light under G. Rose's door. There was none. She was gone for the day. I wondered what she was doing. Was she having dinner with some other guy?

So what if she was, Green Eyes? The two of you weren't exactly high school sweethearts.

I unlocked the door and went into my office. It was pretty well lit from the street lamps, but not well enough to write by.

I left the door open to air the room out, turned on the light, let the cane drop, tossed my coat on the Naugahyde couch and addressed the typewriter.

I rolled the paper up a few inches to recap what I had written so far.

"It started out strictly routine . . ."

It was still there.

Once again, like Dick Powell, I started to write.

"Mr. Hammett, I presume . . ." said a familiar voice from the doorway.

Lieutenant Myron Garter stood there holding a cigar in one hand and a ten- by twelve-inch brown envelope in the other.

"Come in, Myron. Come in. That's what doors are for."

Garter stepped inside and looked around. He stuck the El Producto in his mouth and nodded.

"Not bad, Dashiell. Not bad at all. And handy, just a few blocks from the Beverly Hills station and within scoring distance of some very good restaurants."

"Glad you like it, *mon ami*." Garter hadn't been in the room before. Since I moved in, whenever we met, it was always at headquarters or someplace to eat.

"Quite a view," he said as he walked to the window.

"That it?" I said and pointed to the envelope.

"This is it. The sheet on James Wesley Burke."

I rose and he handed me the envelope.

"Verr-ee In-ter-est-ing," he added.

"Thanks. I'll look it over while we dine. I

141

suppose you've picked the most expensive joint in town. Morton's, LaScala, or maybe The Four Seasons."

"Have to take a raincheck, boycheck."

"How's that?"

"Some police business I have to get back to at the station — and I don't want to rush that extravagant dinner you volunteered."

"Volunteered?" Then I held up the envelope. "Hell, Myron, why didn't you call me? I would have come by and picked this up."

"No strain. I needed to get some fresh air — and pick up some fresh cigars. How's your mom?"

"Fine."

"Your man Burke," Garter pointed at the envelope, "worked for Top Guard Security right here in L.A."

"That so?"

"Yeah. If you're leaving, I'll walk you down the stairs. Protect you from the bogeyman."

"Thanks, but I'll stick around."

Garter moved toward the door leaving a smoke screen behind him. He paused at the threshold and looked back with a William Conrad sneer.

"I thought you were out of the detective business."

"I am."

"Sure you are. Goodnight, shamus." He left, closing the door.

I tossed the envelope on the roll-top and addressed the typewriter. I'd look at the sheet on Burke tomorrow. Tonight I was going to write. I would not fall prey to the distractions that plague the undisciplined wordsmith. Particularly the absent distraction across the hall. I would not let my mind wander and wonder where oh, where had my golden girl gone. That was none of my beeswax, I told myself.

A lady like that, and there were damn few with such beauty, brains and body, must have a swarm of suitors — young and old, rich and richer, bachelors and bamboozlers, who have been stalking around much longer than I, and who probably had a leg up, I was going to say to myself, but switched to head start — on me and my pursuit of The Golden Fleece. Besides, I did have a date with her soon, maybe tomorrow night, so tonight I was going to write.

Sure I was.

I picked up the envelope and pulled out the sheet on James Wesley Burke.

Chapter Fifteen

It didn't take long to read all about the life and times of James Wesley Burke. I already knew about his death. I'll skip most of the boilerplate. He was born in Hattiesburg, Mississippi. Never finished high school. Wanted to be a baseball player. Had a try-out with an Atlanta farm club. Not a bad fielder or runner. As a hitter he had one fault. The curve ball. He couldn't come close. When they found out, the opposing pitchers took unfair advantage of Burke's vulnerability. He struck out so many times that his potential teammates nicknamed him 'kkk' — not after the Klan.

Went to Vietnam. Purple Heart. Head wound. Hospitals overseas, then California. He was never bright to begin with, but his head was never quite the same. Got partial disability. Several jobs, mostly uniformed guard at banks or high-rise buildings but never kept the same job more than a few months. Latest employment with Top Guard Security. Had been there almost two years. A record.

One more thing. James Wesley Burke was married.

As Hercule Poirot might say, *"Cherchez la femme."*

I pulled out my Elgin pocket watch to see if it was too late to go "Cherchezing."

I didn't think so.

Since I couldn't find out anything from Top Guard Security that night, I thought I'd pay a visit to the widow Burke. But first I had to call Lieutenant Garter. Beside the sheet on Burke there was a burglary report on a house on Carmelita left in the envelope he brought over. I thought he might need it that night at the station, so I'd volunteer to drop it off on my way to Genesse Street, James Wesley Burke's last known address.

I called Garter's direct line. When a detective is away from his desk the switchboard picks up on the fourth ring. On ring number four Leslie Reynolds picked up.

"Lieutenant Garter's office. The Lieutenant is not at his desk. May I take a message?"

"Leslie, this is Alex Night. Did Myron go to the can? If he did . . ."

"Hi Alex. No, he's gone for the day. Left about an hour ago. Said he wasn't coming back. Can I take a message?"

"No thanks, Les. No urgency. I'll talk to him in the morning. Goodnight."

"Goodnight."

I thought that was a little strange, I'd swear he made a point of telling me he was going back to the station. Well maybe he changed his mind. I didn't give it much more thought at the time — as least I'd have something to needle him about in the morning. About how he was leading a double life.

My stomach abhors a vacuum, so I stopped at a joint on Wilshire and sucked up a bowl of chili and a Budweiser.

Fifteen minutes later I turned the LeBaron left on LaCienega and headed north on what used to be known as Restaurant Row. There are still some good eating places there, but most of the old places like Cugat's, Tail O' The Cock, Ernest's, Alan Hale's, Ollie Hammond's, are gone or changed hands. What used to be Eddie Arcaro's, an old sports hangout, is now Benihana's.

Ollie Hammond's had been my favorite. A lot of cops and show people stopped there. Open twenty-four hours. You could get the best ham and eggs west of the Pantry any time of the day or night. The split pea soup wasn't bad either. The place was always crowded. After midnight, people would stand for an hour at the bar and get loaded while waiting for a seat.

Old Ollie had a secret. Downstairs he had built a room that looked like a London club. All wood and leather. He'd let the suckers wait upstairs, while only the select few who were in on it went through a secret panel into the pub downstairs. The suckers who waited included some of the biggest stars, writers, producers and directors in town.

As far as I knew the only celebrity he ever told about the room was Frank Sinatra.

When Sinatra went down, had a drink, and looked around, he had the exact same room duplicated in his house right to the last board and bottle.

I used to go there two or three nights a week until Ollie Hammond's mysteriously burned to the ground.

I took a right on Third and headed for Genesse.

It wasn't long before I swung the LeBaron into a restricted zone of an apartment area. I got out, started to take the cane along, but changed my mind and tossed it back into the car. I walked toward a two-story apartment house after verifying the address.

According to the sheet Mrs. Burke's name was Eunice, *nee* McCafferty.

I thought I'd see if the widow Burke was still accepting condolences. If she still lived there.

Well, at least the nameplate was still there. James Burke. I mashed the button. Again. In a half minute there was a buzz then a click at the door. Just like somebody was expecting me.

I pushed the door open and walked into the hallway. I walked up the narrow staircase to the second floor thinking maybe I should have brought along the Malacca. There was no banister. There was hardly any carpet.

When I got there I knocked on the door marked "2G." There were more than a few other marks on the door.

I knocked again. And again.

"Coming! Coming!" A female voice responded from inside. "Take it easy on that door, Sonny."

"Sonny?" I hadn't been called that in a long time. Maybe never.

She swung open the door without looking at who was there and proceeded to go back to a table and pick up her purse.

I took the opportunity to enter, close the door and appraise the territory. The place was lower class messy.

"Greetings," I said.

Eunice turned toward me. A redhead, who fourteen years ago might have danced naked in a strip joint.

But as I looked at her she was dressed, wearing a black lace uplift bra and matching panty. She had also slipped on a black lace see-through negligee.

"Hey," she exclaimed when she turned back toward me. "You're not the pizza man!"

"I'm not?"

There was an awkward pause. In what might be construed as an act of modesty, she dropped her purse on the table and closed up the see-through negligee.

"You're outta here — NOW!"

I smiled my most charming smile and took a step forward.

"Mrs. Burke . . ."

"Out!"

"It is Mrs. Burke, isn't it?"

"Out!" she repeated.

"Eunice." I tried a more familiar approach. "I'd just like to ask you a couple of questions about Jimmy, your husband."

"If you're the fuzz, I've answered all the questions I'm going to . . ."

"It'll just take . . ."

"Mase!" she hollered and looked toward a room to the left of her.

"Look," I said, trying the financial approach, "I've got a hundred-dollar bill . . ."

"You know what you can do with it," spoke a voice as a door opened from what must have been the bathroom.

A man appeared. He was wet and wore a terrycloth robe. But there was something familiar about him.

"You must be Mase," I said.

"You've got ten seconds, Sport."

That cinched it.

This time he was not wearing a ski mask, or a police uniform or a Magnum. But in a flashback three short commands came across my mind:

"Unlock the doors."

"Eyes straight ahead, Sport."

"Shut up!"

If I recognized him, he sure as hell must have made me.

"Five seconds," he said.

"It won't take that long."

For all I knew he was liable to produce that Magnum from under his terrycloth robe and finish what he started on Palm Desert Road.

I walked to the door with as much restraint as I could muster, put my hand around the knob and twisted. But I couldn't resist turning back toward Eunice.

"Is that the latest in widow's weeds?"

As Mase took a step forward I opened the door. Standing there was the pizza man ready to knock.

Another awkward moment.

"Step right in, Sonny," I said. "They're expecting you."

I came out of the apartment house whistling a tuneless tune. I headed toward the LeBaron but something on another car caught my eye. A leftover from the old detective days.

I walked toward the vehicle, a four-door Honda, and studied the windshield. There was a sticker on the lower right side. It was in the form of a shield, stating:

TOP GUARD
SECURITY
1212 N. Bond Ave.
213-463-6375

I took out a pencil and one of my old private investigator cards from my shirt pocket and wrote down the number of the license plate.

I replaced the card and pencil and started to walk away. But I stopped, looked back at the Honda.

"Goodnight, Sport," I said aloud.

"Goodnight," a voice came back.

I looked around. It was the pizza man who passed by behind me and headed for the pizza van.

Well, I had a goodnight's work under my vest, even though I wasn't wearing one. So I went home.

Chapter Sixteen

Now comes the tricky part. In the beginning when I started to set this down, I told you that I'd have to guess at some of the patches in the crazy quilt, the patches that I wasn't actually in.

This is one of those patches. Oh, I know the outcome of all those parts; it's just that I didn't see it all happen and hear the words.

So I've decided to knock off two sap-suckers with one shot. A) To move the events along by telling you what and how things occurred. B) To write it down like I'm going to be doing when I write that first mystery novel. Maybe with a dash of Hammett, a pinch of Chandler and even a smattering of Spillane.

That way you'll get the drift and I'll get the experience — like this.

Eunice stood gobbling a piece of pizza. A sardine slipped from her lip and landed on the upper slope of her left breast. The sardine must have liked it there; it lingered and tried to cohere, but finally slid off and landed on her big toe.

Mason paced like he had just lost the last battle of the Civil War. He came to a halt and threw a fist borrowed from Terminator against an unsuspecting wall. Two cheap prints that hung there rattled.

"Son-of-a-bitch!" Mason squeezed the most out of a familiar phrase with a voice that whiskey had failed to improve. Eunice took another gobble and started talking in the middle of the second bite.

"You think he recognized you without the mask?"

Mason's fist slammed into the wall again, this time leaving an imperfect imprint as well as rattling the cheap prints. And this time one of the frames dropped to the canvas and took the count.

"How the hell do I know?"

"Maybe he didn't."

"And maybe you're Madonna. What the hell's that on your foot?"

"Oh!" Eunice looked down, picked it up and ate it. "Sardine."

"Why the hell did you let him in in the first goddamn place?"

"I thought he was the pizza man, and I was hungry. That's goddamn why."

Mason let that hang. He walked to the table, picked up a wedge of pizza and inhaled a mouthful.

"This tastes like shit."

"Then don't eat it!" Eunice shrugged.

"I won't!"

"Don't. That settles that."

Mason walked to the window and looked down.

"What're you lookin' for?"

"For him. To see if he's still sucking around."

"Is he?" She picked up what was left of Mason's pizza wedge and went to work on it.

"If he is, I can't see him. But if he made me he'll be back. I thought the cops were through nosin' around. I thought it was okay to move in."

"You said he wasn't a real cop."

"He's real enough." Mason pointed to his upper arm. "He gave me this. A few more inches and that slug would have gone through the pump."

"Yeah, I wouldn't want to have lost the both of you."

"What?"

"You and Jimmy."

"Eunice, for chrissakes, get real."

"Okay," Eunice had another bite. "So

what are you gonna do?"

"I'll tell you what I'm gonna do. I'm gonna get a real bankroll and blow."

"What about me?"

"What ABOUT you?"

Mason slowly moved closer. She knew what was coming. She wanted it to happen, like it happened all the times before. Before Burke was dead. When he was dead, and before he was buried. And ever since. She wanted it so bad she could taste it.

"Listen to me baby," he said.

"I'm listening," Eunice hummed.

Mason reached with both hands and lifted the negligee over her pale, freckled shoulders. He let go. It fluttered softly to the floor.

With one hand he put his arm behind her and unsnapped the bustier. It fell. And so did her breasts, but not far. She smiled and swayed her upper body. She knew how.

"I'm listening," she repeated and smiled.

"You think I tossed Burke off that roof just because he might yap? You know damn well why I did it. I'm lookin' at it. And I'd do it again in a minute!"

"He was crazy, Mase — a real nut-case — kept wakin' up at night and slobberin' about Nam. He was crazy . . ."

Mason drew her into his body. He was

built like a gladiator, hard as a radiator and just as hot.

"So am I baby, about you." He kissed her and tasted her tongue and the pizza.

"What're we waiting for?" she said.

"Who's waiting?" Mason lifted her, cradling one arm behind her back, his palm cushioning her salient breast, the other hand under her legs, and started for the bedroom.

Eunice reached back at the table and picked up the last piece of pizza.

That's about how I figure it went.

Chapter Seventeen

How do you spend ten thousand dollars?

I went to Acapulco with Goldie Rose. We stayed at the Las Brisas Hotel. It's one of the ten most popular honeymoon resorts in the world. It's made up of dozens of cabanas spilling down from a mountain that looks across a sparkling bay with sail boats slicing through blue water and with love boats putting to port in the warm harbor.

Each cabana has a pool strewn with orchids. We swam there in the moonlight naked. She wore nothing but her golden earrings. She floated on her back, the clear water washing over the flat of her stomach, lapping onto the swell of her white breasts.

From beneath I surfaced at her side, encircled her in my arms and we drifted down clinging to each other — down — down — down. Until I woke up.

I always was an early riser. Old Army habit. But this was one time I gladly would have made an exception, except I had no choice.

A cold shower brought me completely

back to reality. Three cups of coffee, a slice of rye toast loaded with orange marmalade along with some yogurt and I was on my way to the Hollywood YMCA for the first time since that unpleasantness in Palm Desert.

The Hollywood "Y" is located on Schrader between Selma and Hollywood Boulevard. Recently they spent over nine million bucks renovating — and doubled the dues. Been working out there since I came to town. In the olden, golden days — pre-renovation — a lot of movie stars and gangsters, as well as athletes, frequented the grand old building.

Johnny Weissmuller used to swim there before he became Tarzan, and after. Every day he was in town Bugsy Seigel used to sit in the steam room and let the sweat out of his system, until one night when somebody shot him full of holes and let the blood out of his system.

Lee Marvin was a regular and the old timers still talk about Charles Bronson and those one-handed push-ups. He could do more with one hand than anybody else could do with two. Probably still can. Current regulars include Santa Claus and Gil Grissum: CSI. Tim Allen and Bill Petersen.

Since it was my first time back I eased into

things by halving my usual routine while the usual kibitzers asked the usual questions about the recently acquired ballistic imprint on my left shank. My answers were worthy of at least an "honorable mention" at a Liars Club contest.

After the workout I stopped over at Celebrity Car Wash on Vine Street and had the LeBaron cleaned and pressed. While I waited, I called Garter on his direct line. He was at his desk having breakfast, at least his second, maybe his third. I asked him how long it would take to run a make on the Honda plate.

"Not long," he replied and went about his bagel.

"Could you chew that a little finer?" I asked.

"What do you mean by that?" he remarked.

I guess he thought I was referring to the bagel.

"I mean how long? Five minutes? Ten? Twenty?"

"Sold!" he cracked.

"Come on, Myron, be serious."

"Okay. Now you've got serious. Call me back in five."

I got some more change from Wilma the pretty cashier, then swapped a couple of jokes with Joe, the not so pretty manager.

By then I figured Garter must be finished with the bagel and the make on the Honda.

I was right on both counts.

"Alex, your Japanese beetle is registered to a Frank Mason employed at Top Guard Security, 1212 Bond Avenue. Is that a coincidence — or what?"

"I'd say it's 'or what.' By the way, old dick, what's with that bullshit about working late at the office last night? You got some fox on the string you're afraid to introduce me to? Think she might . . ."

"Sometime," he interrupted, "you ought to learn how to mind your own business, asshole!"

The phone went dead and so did I, damn near. It wasn't just what he said, but the way he said it. He wasn't clowning. I had never heard that tone in his voice before. Not when he was talking to me. The truth is I was hurt. I was as close to Myron Garter as I was to anybody in my life.

Whatever it was, I'd let him cool off first, then straighten things out, no matter what I had to do to do it.

It was a warm clear day in Southern California, so I put the top down on my shiny gray LeBaron, pushed the radio dial to KGRB and headed southeast toward Bond Avenue while Keely Smith wailed out the lyrics to "Down Around the River" with her then-husband Louis Prima providing the musical background.

But along the way I couldn't help thinking about Eunice, the erstwhile strip dancer who had changed partners and was now dancing with good ol' Mase who just happened to work at the same stand where her deceased husband once toiled.

I wondered if the three of them had a lot of fun together in the good old days before the Palm Desert expedition.

I wondered if they went to movies together, and bowling and balling.

I wondered a lot of things. I always was a curious sort. They say that curiosity killed the cat. But what the hell do I care. I'm not a cat.

Keely was finished. Nat King Cole started singing "Unforgettable"; and you bet he was. And is.

I pulled into the parking lot alongside the Top Guard Security building on Bond. In so doing I drove right past the sign that said:

TOP GUARD SECURITY
Parking for
Top Guard Security Vehicles
ONLY
Others park at your own risk

162

I took the risk. Nobody shot at me, or even shouted at me. I walked past several vehicles with shields on the door panels and windshields emblazoned with the company logo. I walked into the cement block building.

The woman at the reception desk reminded me of a waitress I used to know who reminded me of Mercedes McCambridge. Her voice sounded like an anti-cigarette ad, but she wasn't smoking at the moment. I was.

I played it charming and handed her one of my old cards, saying that I'd like to talk to whomever was in charge of personnel.

"Why?" she inquired logically enough.

I waltzed around verbally, with something about a matter of "professional courtesy."

She shrugged, took my card and walked through the door leading inside. A couple of minutes later she came back.

"Mr. Quigley said to wait."

I waited. Pretty damn close to half an hour. Two-and-a-half cigarettes to be exact.

Finally her buzzer buzzed and she picked up the phone and listened for five seconds.

"Mr. Quigley says you can go in now. Second on the right. His name's on the door."

So it was. The door was open so I walked

in. Mr. Quigley did not rise or offer his hand. He wore an expression that went with a gallows. It looked as if his left ear had slipped a little and he appeared in need of a Bloody Mary to match his eyeballs. A classic hangover if I ever saw one. He barely moved in the three minutes I stayed there.

I told him I was doing a credit check on one of his employees, Frank Mason, and I'd appreciate a little information . . .

He cut me short saying that Frank Mason no longer worked at Top Security. He quit about two weeks ago. Mr. Quigley made it plain that the audience was over. I took the hint, but paused at the doorway saying that I hoped he had a good time last night.

He was not amused. But then neither was I. I had traded half an hour of my valuable time for something I could have found out over the phone, except that over the phone people aren't prone to provide the sort of information I had hoped to get.

I bade the receptionist a good day and went about my business. But I should have paid heed to the warning about parking "at your own risk."

I don't know where birds go to die, but I'll tell you where they go to shit. On my car.

For other people they sing.

Chapter Eighteen

I stopped in at Mrs. Kramer's and got four packs of Luckies and a six-minute lecture on the ineluctable consequences of cigarette smoking. Mrs. Kramer was winding down with "Alex, for the last time I'm telling you . . ."

"You sure it's the last time?"

"Don't be a smart ass . . ."

"I apologize!"

"Accepted — smoke the damn pipes, you'll last longer — you got any tobacco left?"

"Some."

"Smoke it. That's the last pack of cigarettes I'm going to sell you and the last I'm going to say on the subject. Any questions?"

"Yes, tell me about Goldie Rose."

"She's a nice girl."

"How nice?"

"She's too damn good . . ."

Damn the fates. In walked three women, friends as well as customers of Mrs. Kramer's, and that effectively put the quietus on our conversation. By the time I made it to the door they were on the subject, or subjects, of somebody's breast implants.

When I got to the hallway of the WRITERS AND ARTISTS BUILDING, the Bickersons were at it again.

"The trouble with you, Elliott," Morgan Noble was saying, "is that you've let failure go to your head."

"Put quite simply, Madam Ovary . . ."

"Simply, is the only way you could put it . . ."

". . . you are a common thief."

"I am not a common anything."

"I repeat a thief, and the next time I catch you snatching my trade papers, I'll . . ."

"Stamp your foot?"

"I'll report you to my friend Henry Fenenbock . . ."

"Elliott, you don't have any friends, except at the Hollywood Wax Museum."

"I give you fair warning, my murky one, tampering with another's mail is a federal offense. Keep your cutpurse fingers off my *Variety* and *Reporter*. If you are indigent, and that would be a noteworthy reflection on the good taste of the book-buying public, I will happily pay for a subscription. I don't want your piratical imprints on my periodicals — or anyplace else."

"I was just hoping to find your obituary in today's edition. You probably would rate no more than three lines."

"Madam, I have no intention of predeceasing you. As a matter of fact I vow, here and now, to piss on your grave."

"You mean dribble, don't you, Elliott?"

"You'll find out when your remains are awash with my fluid . . ."

"Good morning," I interrupted, and was saved the necessity of saying something clever when I heard the phone ringing inside my office. I fumbled for my key, got the door open, left it open and strode toward the phone. I dropped my Malacca, picked up the phone and in the process also dropped the receiver. I retrieved it and greeted the caller.

"Hello," I grumbled. "Alex Night."

"Alex," came my mother's voice. "You sound out of breath and out of sorts. Are you okay?"

"Sure, Mom. I'm fine. How about you? How's everything?"

I expected a generally affirmative answer and a reasonably short one. My mother is not a complainer and usually not long-winded. This time was an exception. She proceeded to tell me that she thought she was getting old and absent-minded. Last night she couldn't remember where she had put a letter from her cousin Irene Poletes. Cousin Irene had moved from Athens to Volos because Athens was too smoggy and crowded. My mother couldn't find the new address because she wanted to write and tell cousin Irene she might take a trip to Greece and pay a visit next summer since cousin Irene's husband Petros had died from the cancer and all of her kids had grown up and moved away and besides they hadn't seen each other since the two of them were kids themselves. But she found the letter this morning — it was in a magazine — but why couldn't she remember that last night? Could it be the first sign of Alzheimer's?

"I don't think so, Mom." I lit a Lucky. That was a mistake because that gave her a chance to tell me what was going on over at Larchmont Village since I moved out of the old office.

Two of the shops had gone out of business because of the high rents and Jerry the barber met her on the street and told her that Mr. Simms got married and it's only been three months since his wife of thirty-six years, Adrienne, has been dead.

"Mom," I interrupted as gently as I knew how, "I'm a little busy right now. I'll call you later on. Okay?"

"Sure. How's the new office?"

"Fine."

"And the leg?"

"Fine . . . look, Mom . . ."

"I know, you're busy . . . by the way, Alex, have you finished the novel yet?"

I looked at the sheet still on the roller of the typewriter with the same sentence on the same page.

"Not yet, Mom . . . that's why I've got to get back to work . . ."

"Good. Alex . . ."

"Yes, Mom?"

"That novel, it doesn't have a lot of dirty stuff in it, does it? Like the 'f' word?"

"Dirty stuff? Hell no, Mom . . ."

"Well you better put some in — or nobody'll buy it. And sex, Alex. Sex sells. People expect that today. You don't want to be labeled old fashioned."

"I'll do that, Mom."

"Alex, have you seen Myron lately?"

She hit a nerve, but I didn't want to say anything to her about Garter's early morning reference to her only son as an asshole.

"See him all the time, Mom. He's fine. Talked to him this morning. I was just going to call him, maybe have lunch."

"Tell him to go easy on the calories. He's

putting on too much weight."

"I will . . ."

"And tell him I say hello and to come over and have dinner . . ."

"I will. So long, Mom."

I hung up the phone. Looked at the typewriter, then looked back at the phone again. I picked it up and walked over to the Naugahyde couch, letting the long telephone line trail behind. I lay on the couch and balanced the phone on my stomach.

I had to call Myron. By now he had cooled off as much as he was going to, even though I didn't know exactly what I had said that ticked him off; although I knew it was something about last night. And I knew I couldn't get anything done until whatever was wrong between us got settled. Whatever it was, I was ready to eat humble pie. Myron Garter and Alex Night went back a long way. Back to the Academy.

Back to the Academy a passel of years ago. I had stopped in Los Angeles on my way from Nam to Akron, but I never did get back to Akron. I decided to trade in the sleet, the snow and the stink for sunshine and citrus.

I listened to an announcement on radio station KMPC that said the police department was looking for a few good men and the next thing I knew I was in line at the Academy standing in front of a guy named Myron Garter. I guess it was fate or destiny or chance that jumbled us up and tossed us together in the first place, but after that it just seemed that we gravitated toward each other through the testing and training.

Garter was a native Angeleno, graduated from Fairfax High and Cal State Northridge. He was engaged to Rhoda Green, his high school sweetheart. We both made it through the Academy, Myron very near the top of the class — he was a serious student — and I very near the middle of the class. I was faking the whole damn thing largely because I wasn't sure I wanted to be a cop in the first place. My dad hadn't given up trying to convince me to come back to dear ol' Akron and run the saloon while he vacationed four months of the year in Florida.

The day we graduated from the Academy Myron and Rhoda were married and I was best man.

Garter and I both got assigned to the Rampart Division, but since we were both rookies we each had a different senior partner. Someday we wanted to work together. Talked about it all the time at the station and on our days off when we'd take off for the desert or Arrowhead. He with Rhoda, of course, and I with a variety of sugar and spice. In those days the fear of AIDS had not reared its ugly head and men and women went to bed together because it was unfriendly not to. In the course of their bedding Rhoda became pregnant and there weren't any two happier people from the desert to the sea — until she lost the baby and the doctor, make that doctors, said not much chance for any more.

Then one night fate or destiny or chance tossed Myron and me together again. Both our cruisers responded to a prowler radio report. Myron and his partner got there just ahead of us.

An armed prowler had been spotted and was still in the apartment building. He was young and he panicked and fired a couple of shots when a tenant, also with a gun, spotted him. Myron had gone around back and his partner waited in front for back up.

There were a couple more shots from inside so I flew in while my partner covered the rear and Garter's partner stayed out in front. I'll skip the details but just put it down to breaking in the wrong door. When I heard more gunshots from the rooftop I smashed through the door of what I thought was a dark and empty apartment to get to the outside fire escape. The apartment was dark all right, but not empty. A respected married citizen was in the bedroom making love to his kept woman while the respected married citizen's wife thought he was out of town for the weekend.

Meanwhile, I got to the window and the fire escape and made it to the roof where Myron and the young prowler were making like *High Noon* at midnight.

I snuck up from behind and shot the young sonofabitch in the leg. He dropped his gun, went to his knees and prayed to God and Myron and me not to kill him. We didn't.

The press, including a live camera crew from KTLA, got there and took pictures and made tape. The respected citizen's wife I.D.'d the husband from either the pictures or the tape or both, and he went from hot springs to hot water.

For some reason he blamed me for the entire affair. He filed a complaint and the lieutenant had no choice but to take it upstairs to Internal Affairs. I had no choice but to tell the lieutenant to go to hell. Myron and the other officers came to my defense but the respected citizen demanded satisfaction. His wife demanded a divorce.

I would have gotten only a reprimand but my Greek temper got the better or worse of me and I quit. As I said, too many rules, just like the Army — only I wasn't drafted into the police force. I had volunteered in and so I volunteered out. I went into the private detective business where I could make my own rules — more or less. A few weeks later Myron Garter got a chance to join the Beverly Hills Police Department. He never forgot that I raced up that fire escape to help him. But I knew, and still know, he would have done the same for me.

Yes, Myron Garter and Alex Night went back a long way.

I dialed Myron's direct number.

"Lieutenant Garter," he answered.

"Myron, this is Alex the asshole, don't hang up . . ."

"Alex . . ."

"Whatever it was I said, however it was that I was out of line, I'm sorry. I apologize. Come over and slug me or boot me in the balls or set me on fire. I promise to mind my own business so long as we both shall live."

Silence. Dead air.

Well, Night, I thought to myself, to paraphrase that line from *Casablanca* — this could be the end of a beautiful friendship.

But it wasn't.

"No, Alex, I'm the one who was out of line. Something happened. Never mind what it was. It doesn't matter anymore. It's over and done with and forgotten — if that's okay with you."

He might as well've hit me with a left hook. I was staggered. Speechless.

Silence. Dead air.

"Alex . . . ?"

"Yeah, sure, Myron."

"All right then," he suddenly was the old Myron Garter again. "Anything else on that peanut brain?"

"Have you eaten?" I couldn't think of anything else to say.

"Just thinking about it."

"Come on over. I'll buy . . ."

"Just a minute, this doesn't take the place of that expensive dinner . . ."

"Hell no. This is an added perk. There's something I want to fill you in on . . ."

"I thought you were out of the detective business."

"I am, but you're not. How'd you like to crack the Burke murder?"

"Not my case. Not my jurisdiction."

"Come on over anyhow, you just might be a hero."

"You mean like in sandwich? I'll see you."

I never felt better in my life!

It was as if I had found a long lost brother, even though it had only been a little more than a couple of hours. I still wondered what it was that bothered Myron in the first place, and if there was anything I could do . . . but right then and there I gave myself a silent lecture and reprimand. Butt out, Kyrios Nyktas, that's what got you in the barrel in the first place. If and when the time comes and he wants you to know, he'll tell you, so shut the hell up and write that damn book.

I started to rise but the telephone on my belly rang. I lay there and answered it.

"Hello."

"Night, I been trying to reach you all morning. First no answer, then busy . . ."

"Who is this?"

"Petey."

"What do you want?"

"I want to do you a favor, that's what. Bull Connors is coming after you . . ."

"Who the hell is Bull Connors?"

"Jesus Christ, Night! He's the guy you called 'Moose' — the guy whose skull you cracked. Word got around about what you done to him and he says he's gonna get even."

"So?"

"So he's out of the hospital and says he's gonna get you — he's gone bananas. Now get the hell out of there and call the cops now! This minute!"

I rose to a sitting position.

". . . I'm telling you, Night, he's a maniac and don't forget who called you . . ."

I felt a presence. I looked toward the open door. The doorway was filled with Moose Malloy, a.k.a. Bull Connors. His head was bandaged. There was murder in his eye . . . mine. He looked at me the way a lion looks at a lamb, a big fish looks at a little fish, a grizzly at honey. He was the bad news bear.

"Night . . . Night, are you there?" Petey's voice came through the phone.

"I'm here . . . thanks."

I hung up the phone and thought things over — for about a tenth of a second. It's funny; the things you can think of in a tenth of a second — when your life hangs in the balance. You know, the old saw about your whole life flashing before you.

Take it easy, Night, I said to myself, giving myself a pep talk. You've been in tougher spots than this. You'll think of something, you always did over in Nam when you won the war single handed and taught those Commies not to screw around with democracy. When you were on the force and wiped out all the crime in Los Angeles while leaning against bullets, when you set a new standard in the field of private investigation.

Right now you're only up against one man. He puts his pants on one leg at a time. It's true that his leg is as big as King Kong's, but so what? And he's hurt. Look at that bandage on his bean. He might collapse any time. And he's dumb. Why he's so dumb that he probably thinks you're scared shitless.

I was.

That all took place in a tenth of a second. In the second tenth of a second I glanced from Bull Connors to the cane on the floor.

"Not a chance, paly." Mr. Connors knew just what I was thinking. But he was thinking something else.

He stepped inside and closed the door. It was the sound of impending doom. The sound was deafening, until he spoke. But before he spoke, he lifted a sap from his right rear pocket.

"I'm gonna give you a paint job."

Chapter Nineteen

Bull Connors whacked the sap into his plentiful palm and took one step forward.

"Bull," I said in an effort to ease the tension. "You mind if I smoke?"

It didn't work.

"You'll smoke all right," he said. "Your feets' already in the fire."

"Bull, you're a reasonable man, a businessman. Why do this? There's nothing in it for you."

"Yes there is."

"What?"

"Satisfaction."

"Oh, that."

"You made me look foolish to my friends. You cracked my head."

"I'll apologize. I'll tell your friends I snuck up on you, hit you from behind. Besides, Bull, it was self defense. I didn't come to see you, you came to see me, remember? You and that putz, Petey Boyle . . ."

"No more talk," he said, and I knew he meant it.

179

The events of the next few minutes are jumbled. The fight itself, blows and counter blows, are a bit hazy. I've known fighters in the ring to have the same experience, win or lose. They can't remember the physical encounter itself, but they can tell you what the trainer in the corner said and what the lady in the third row was wearing and swearing.

Suffice it to say sounds of warfare penetrated through the walls and into the hallway and warrens of the venerable structure. Glass breaking — objects being thrown — bodies banging against walls, mostly my body — grunts — groans — collisions — kicks, and all manner of Herculean combat, all ignoring the rules and regulations of the Marquis of Queensbury.

Somehow I did manage to gain possession of my Malacca and fend off some of the blows of Bull's sap. But it was like trying to ward off a raging bull with a feather boa.

Outside, writers had come forth from their warrens, no doubt welcoming the interruption as writers always do.

I could hear somebody hollering: "Call the cops!"

"Right," I hollered back. "Call the cops!"

That's when our entwined bodies, Bull's and mine, burst through the door with cannonball velocity. The spectators wisely retreated as the carnage continued.

Now here's the strange part. While I don't have a clear recollection of the fight, I have a rather vivid memory of the curious dialogue that accompanied the encounter. The dialogue was not between Bull and me. The talking phase of our relationship had ended.

But the spectators included E. Elliott Elliot, Morgan Noble, Wes Weston, the Bernstein brothers — Bruce and Bernie — and Goldie Rose. The commentary was among them. I must say that among the gallery, Morgan Noble gave evidence of near euphoria. In fact this probably was as close to climaxing as she had come in years. It went something like this:

Wes. "I'll take the big guy and give six to one."

Elliott. "Typical Texas mentality."

Wes. "Any takers?"

Goldie. "For God's sake, somebody do something before he gets killed." By "he" I assumed she meant me.

Morgan. "I've seen better fights in movies."

Elliott. "At porno houses, no doubt."

Wes. "Best movie fight I can recollect was between Duke Wayne and Randy Scott in *The Spoilers*."

Morgan. "Wrong. You could spot Scott's

double in that one. The fight between them in Pittsburgh was better — in the mine shaft and the elevator."

Bruce. "What about *The Adventures of Martin Eden*? The one between . . ."

Bernie. ". . . Glenn Ford and Ian Mac-Donald."

Wes. "That was good. But how about Greg Peck and Chuck Heston in *The Big Country*?"

Morgan. "Bullshit! Who the hell could believe that bony Peck could beat up hulk Heston?"

Bruce. "Peck had to win . . ."

Bernie. ". . . he produced the picture."

Goldie. "For God's sake, somebody do something!"

All the while Bull was wildly swinging his sap and I was countering with the cane until the cane snapped from impact on Bull's forearm. But Bull did drop the sap.

I glanced at the stub of my cane, tossed it away and charged the stunned Bull with a volley of lefts and rights.

Goldie turned to someone who was now standing next to her.

"Call the police," she said.

"I am the police," Myron Garter replied.

"Then do something!" Goldie suggested.

Both Bull and I were now on the floor.

Bull had the advantage. He was on top. I don't know which part of me hurt the most, my head which had taken several punches from Bull's iron cantaloupe fists, my shoulders and arms which had absorbed the sap shots, my ribs which I'm sure must have cracked again, or my shin which felt like I had been shot there again. I was about to give up and allow myself the welcome relief of being beaten to death when Myron swung into action.

He didn't exactly swing.

Myron Garter moved — not fast, not slow — he picked up the fallen sap, hauled back with all his strength and slugged Bull Connors across the bandaged skull. This resulted in two sounds, the sharp crack of bone rupturing inside Bull's head and the dull thud of Bull's body settling onto the floor of the hallway. I can not remember the sound of two more welcomed sounds.

"How's that?" Garter said, looking at Goldie.

"That's good," she responded.

The spectators, all show business people, must have agreed because they burst into spontaneous applause, all but Wes Weston.

By now two uniformed Beverly Hills policemen had climbed the stairs and joined the party. Immediately they recognized

Lieutenant Myron Garter.

"Lieutenant," said one of the officers. "How'd you get here so fast? We just got the call."

"That's why I'm a lieutenant." Garter pointed to Bull Connors who amazingly was already stirring. Almost anybody else would have been out for a week, or dead. "Book this one."

"Yes, sir," snapped one of the constables.

The two officers went about the assignment. It wasn't easy. They cuffed Connors, hands behind his back, half lifted, half dragged him to his feet. He swayed like a bleary Buddha, but kept his balance.

"What's the charge?" asked the other constable.

"Destruction of property, mayhem, assault with a deadly weapon." Garter slapped the sap into the officer's palm, then looked at me as I struggled to my feet with the aid of Goldie Rose and E. Elliott Elliot. "This guy have anything to do with the Burke killing?"

I was going to say he damn near had something to do with my killing but at that moment I couldn't have said it even if I tried. I settled for shaking my head "no."

"Too bad," Garter said to me, then to the officers, "move him out."

The two officers convoyed Mr. Connors toward the stairs as the spectators cleared a pathway.

"Alex . . ." Goldie touched my broken cheek.

"Goldie, please don't ask me if I'm all right."

"I won't, but . . . are you?"

"No. Lieutenant Myron Garter, Beverly Hills Police, this is Goldie Rose, writer type."

"Hi," smiled Myron.

"Lieutenant," Elliot extended his hand. "I am E. Elliott Elliot, also a writer type and as a citizen of Beverly Hills I commend you on your expedient action."

"Thank you," said Myron as they shook, then he looked at me. "I don't suppose you feel like lunch?"

"Pass," I said.

"Call me when your head clears."

"Sure thing."

Myron Garter walked away, to have lunch I suppose.

"Get him into my rooms," Elliot ordered. "I have a first aid kit."

I was surprised by two things. First, this was the only time I ever remembered seeing E. Elliott Elliot without his walking stick. I think he even took it into the toilet with him.

The other thing that surprised me, although I guess it shouldn't have, was the conversation that went on among my fellow writers as we were leaving. It went about like this:

Wes. "I still say the big fella would've whipped him."

Bruce. "Whipped him, hell . . ."

Bernie. ". . . he would've murdered him."

Morgan. "What about the fight between Wayne and Forrest Tucker in *Chisum*?" That was great."

Wes. "Well, the fight wasn't that great but I liked the part when Tucker fell off the balcony and landed on the bull's horn . . ."

That's all I remember, or want to remember, as Goldie and Elliot led what was left of me into Elliot's suite.

Chapter Twenty

Elliot occupied two adjoining rooms, which he had converted at great expense and refurbished in the fashion of a Victorian Club. Like Elliot himself, it reflected another era, proud and courtly, debonair and dead. Too bad.

Elliot broke out his first aid kit, which I'm sure had never been used until then, and as I reposed on an oversized leather chair Goldie with the hands of an angel made ministrations on my assorted bruises, while triple E retrieved his walking stick and watched with an amused air.

I had been attended by nurses many times, from the tough and tender saviors of Vietnam to Oliver Hardy in Palm Desert, but never before had I felt such a soothing, healing benediction.

I'll always remember the welcomed touch of Goldie's hands and the droning sounds of Elliot's unwelcomed epigrams. I wasn't paying much attention — to him.

"Bravo, my boy — best brawl I've seen

since a little set-to at Ciro's — 1955 I believe it was, between my then employer Darryl F. Zanuck and some unremembered trombone player. Darryl destroyed both the musician and his instrument. Big fellow he was too, not Zanuck, the musician. Not as big as your opponent, but then who is? Bravo! And your friend the lieutenant, he restores a citizen's faith in law enforcement. And don't concern yourself about the damage. I'll square it with the landlord, we're old chums, Henry and I. I have been his most prestigious and prized tenant lo these many years. My only regret is that I didn't purchase the building myself so that I might have the satisfaction of evicting Madam Ovary."

"Now Elliott, you enjoy your little skirmishes with Morgan," said Goldie. "Admit it."

"I'll admit no such thing, and I will particularly not admit her across my threshold. Have you seen her room? Inviting as a skunk hole, but then of course it is, since it is inhabited by a skunk. I may circulate a petition to have her ousted. Would you sign it, Goldie?"

"No."

"Nice set-up you've got here, Elliot," I said, trying to steer the conversation away from the madam.

"And why not?" Elliot was at the sideboard pouring from a crystal decanter. "For forty-odd years I made a fortune writing and re-writing the same story with only the names changed to preserve my illustrious reputation and extravagant lifestyle."

"Are you serious?" I smiled.

"Dead serious. And I'm not the only one. Many of the old writing fraternity did the same, only they lacked my panache. Borden Chase for one comes to mind. Look at the pictures he wrote and re-wrote, mostly westerns — *Red River*, *Vera Cruz*, *Bend of the River*, *Lone Star*, *Man From Colorado*, *Tycoon* — same plot with a slight variation. Either two friends become adversaries then become friends again — or two adversaries become friends, then become adversaries again in the final showdown. He was a good writer but never troubled himself much thinking up an original plot. And why should he? The studio was perfectly satisfied and so were the viewers, as are the viewers today who watch television. Numbskull nourishment. And why not? Since the networks are run mainly by numbskulls. Insensitive toddlers who are anxious to give you the benefit of their weeks of experience."

"You feel the same way about novels, Elliott?" Goldie asked as I savored the touch of her hand.

"As far as I am concerned, my friend W. Somerset Maugham was the last novelist. Would either of you care for a drink? Brandy? Scotch? Bourbon? Gin or vodka?"

"Don't think so," I said rubbing my neck.

"I'll have a straight scotch," said Goldie.

"Today's novelists," Elliot continued as he went about the business of Goldie's drink, "are about as serious as Sunday painters. 'Of all these arts in which the wise excel, Nature's chief masterpiece is writing well.' "

"Is that one of your couplets, Elliott?" Goldie was closing up the first aid kit.

"No. John Shefield, Duke of Buckinghamshire. But then, what's the point of writing well today? There's no demand for it. Nobody reads. So like the eagle I shall suffer little birds to sing. Here's your scotch. Glenlivet satisfactory?"

"Very satisfactory, thanks." Goldie turned toward me. "Confusion to the enemy."

"Yeah, but first you've got to figure out who the enemy is. Thanks for the repairs. Sorry to keep you from your quota today . . ."

"It's okay, I just finished *The Case of the Wholesome Whore*."

"Congratulations — and what are you working on, Elliot?"

I could have sworn that at that instant Goldie sipped her scotch in order to suppress a smile.

"At the moment, my fustian fellow, I am between scenarios. A temporary aberration, mind you."

"Elliott has several very good ideas. He's told me about them," said Goldie.

"Yes. You see I've been blessed with the ingrained ability to construct an uncluttered sentence and with an uncanny ear for sophisticated dialogue."

"I see," I said.

"Unfortunately, uncluttered sentences and sophisticated dialogue are no longer in vogue."

"Fortunately, Elliott invested heavily in real estate."

"True. However, if good taste and eloquence ever return to this benighted profession, you can be assured of my prominent resurgence."

"I'm sure of that, Elliot," I rose uncertainly with Goldie's help. "And I thank you for the use of the first aid kit and the hall."

"You want me to drive you home?" Goldie volunteered.

"No thanks, I'll just go lie down on my couch for a while." Goldie took the last sip of Glenlivet and escorted me to the door. "Thanks again, Elliot."

"*Noblesse oblige,* dear boy." Elliot sniffed at his brandy from its snifter. "*Noblesse oblige.*"

Elliot closed the door behind us and Goldie and I moved down and across the hall toward my office.

"Mr. Elliot," I said, "is a man who has conclusive opinions on just about any given subject."

"That he does. But I don't know if he'll ever write so much as another word."

"I know the feeling . . ."

"None of the younger people who run the studios even remember him, and of course he won't touch television — or vice versa."

"At least they won't have to throw any charity bazaars for him."

"Hardly, and he does know everybody and everything that goes on in Beverly Hills — a real busybody and buttinsky — but with a heart of gold."

"Like *The Wholesome Whore*? Say what is it with you and whores anyhow? You seem to know an awful lot about them . . ."

"I do."

"How come?"

"Did a little social work with 'Children of the Night' . . ."

"Know what?"

"What?"

"You're aces."

"So are you, even if you are a little crazy."

"As Norman Bates observed, 'Everybody's a little crazy.' "

We stopped in front of my office. Only the splintered framework of the door remained. I twisted the knob, opened the wreckage, walked inside, closed it behind me and waved through the fragmented frame to my Nightingale.

"Don't forget," I said. "We've still got that date now that you've put *The Wholesome Whore* to bed."

"You better go to bed yourself. I'll see you later."

"I'll see you in my dreams, I hope."

"By the way," she said, "if you need anything, just whistle. I'll be right across the hall."

I stood there watching as she turned and walked into her office. She didn't have Bette Davis eyes but she did have Betty Grable legs. Mind you Betty Grable was long before my time and so was Bette Davis but I do watch those old movies on American Movie Classics so I'm pretty up to date on what's out of date.

I turned and surveyed the mess in my office. Miraculously about the only thing that hadn't been damaged was the typewriter. I had no excuse for not writing the novel except for the way that I felt. That was excuse enough.

With pained effort I bent down, picked the phone and its displaced receiver off the floor. I rested the receiver on the cradle, then lifted the receiver to hear if there was a dial tone. There was. Then I decided to take no calls. I put the phone and the receiver on the desk separately.

I picked up a displaced Naugahyde pillow from the floor and placed it on the Naugahyde couch.

Then I lay upon the couch — gingerly. I needed to get some sleep. That's it, sleep, perchance to dream. Maybe I could even pick up my dream where Goldie and I left off — naked in that orchid-strewn pool in Acapulco.

But my thoughts strayed to Petey Boyle. I wouldn't have put it past Petey to have sicced Bull Connors on me — and then call. That way — no matter which of the two of us came out ahead — so would Petey, the little putz.

But at that moment I just didn't care. With my last conscious effort I steered my thoughts and desires back to Goldie Rose.

I only partially succeeded. In my mind there ensued a stylized, slow motion montage with some of the images stretched and slanted right out of one of those UFA Fatherland films like *The Cabinet of Dr. Caligari* or *Metropolis*.

There was Goldie Rose all right — a.k.a. Trig Barker and John Grim — but she was in that famous Sins of Cinema poster depicting all the Hays Office movie taboos of the thirties and forties.

She was half dressed in a black silk skimpy outfit with a smoking cigarette and gun pointing down at a slain policeman with his head leaking blood. She was showing a lot of cleavage and inner thigh.

Other taboos were in evidence: an empty whiskey glass in her other hand, and on the nearby round table a bottle of booze and a hypodermic needle.

There was a Tommy gun across the cop's corpse and at his elbow playing cards, aces and eights. His badge number was sixty.

Then there were scenes from the robbery and pursuit in Palm Desert — stretched and twisted — punctuated by gunshots fired by the counterfeit cops and by me — and the reverberating echoes of more gunshots.

I was on the moors calling for Nora and being answered by sirens and searchlights and the lovely face of Cynthia Alderdyce.

I was in a hospital dancing with Zsa Zsa, but I tripped and was falling from a high place — but lucky for me, the face on the falling body turned into somebody else, somebody wearing a skin-colored ski mask and a police uniform. He was oozing blood like the cop in the Sins of Cinema poster.

They were scraping him off the sidewalk, then the sign painter was scraping my name off a frosted glass door.

And then my name was on another door — and standing there, smiling, was the girl of my dreams. No, not you, Nora. Too bad. You had your chance. This girl was Goldie and she was real. Except when I put my arms around her I was embracing vapor. Goldie was gone.

I was looking at a certified check for ten big ones — lovely big round circles, but not as big and as round as Miss Sweden. She put her arms around me to kiss me — but the kiss turned into a peck on the cheek from Mrs. Alderdyce — or was it my mother?

Myron was enjoying my mother's Avgolemonou soup and so was I until he dumped his bowl over my head.

When I wiped the soup out of my eyes there was Mase coming toward me — he turned into Bull Connors — with a sap swinging in slow motion.

And then there was Goldie in that Sins of Cinema poster again — only she turned into the widow Burke eating a pizza with a sardine slipping onto her bare breast and loving it — with Mr. Mase glaring at me — so was the Magnum in his mitt.

Now here comes the tricky part again — another one of those patches in the crazy quilt — another patch that I wasn't in but pieced together from subsequent events.

While I lay there recuperating on the Naugahyde couch trying to make sense of what had already happened — while also trying to dream up an erotic vision of Goldie Rose — Mr. Mase was dreaming up a scheme of his own. It must have gone something like this:

Eunice Burke's apartment did not look any better in the daytime, in fact it looked worse. And so did she. The cruel light of day accented the faint road map of wrinkles on her face and the tatty texture of her skin,

197

which took on an egg yolk glow in the flush of the afternoon. Still the body of work was voluptuous and in ample evidence thanks to the deeply divided, short-length, clinging kimono she was wearing. That's all she was wearing.

Frank Mason wore tan work pants with a loosened belt and an undershirt that failed to cover swirling tufts of dark hair on his upper body.

Eunice was spooning strawberry yogurt out of a carton. Mason was on the telephone in the middle of a conversation.

". . . because I'm getting some heat. What kind of heat? Cop heat. No, nobody knows anything about you. Not yet, but you want to keep it that way, don't you? Good, because when I get heat, we all get heat.

"It's that dick, Night. I'll tell you when I see you and that'll be tonight, eleven o'clock, your office. It can be handled, but make sure your partner's there too . . ."

Mase winked at Eunice.

". . . and tell him to bring five thousand dollars."

Eunice came closer and stuck a spoonful of yogurt in Mase's mouth.

". . . because I'm leaving town," Mase said through the mouthful of yogurt. "And I need five G's. That was Burke's share anyhow."

Eunice tried to stick another spoon of yogurt in Mase's face, but he waved her away.

"Both of you be there — with the dough. We've got to talk. You do understand, don't you, Mr. Fedona?"

Mase hung up.

"Mr. Fedona understands." Mase smiled as Eunice shoved some yogurt into his smile.

"You call that a bankroll?" She sneered, "Where the hell are we going? Tijuana?"

"You know something, Eunice? You got a lot of things going for you, but brains isn't one of them things."

"Yeah? And I suppose you're some aerospace engineer?"

"Yeah, in a way I am, cause I'm engineering us right out of this pesthole into a life of leisure and luxury."

"I'll believe it when I see it!"

"You'll see it all right. I know exactly what I'm doing and I'm doing the thinking for the both of us."

"Okay, but don't strain that great brain of yours."

"No strain, baby. First of all I know a joint where I can lay low for a while."

"How long a while?"

"Not long." He picked up a pad and

pencil from the telephone table. "Here's a number where you can call me if something comes up . . ."

"Why can't I come with you now?"

". . . but don't use this phone to call me. If the cops come back and I'm not here, they're liable to bug it."

"I said, why can't I come with you now?"

"Because I got to set this up and I can't be carrying extra baggage . . ."

"Is that what I am? Extra goddamn baggage?"

"That ain't what I mean and you know it . . ."

"You wouldn't be thinking of just leaving me here behind would you, Mase? Cause if you are . . ."

"Are you nuts, after all we been through? It's you and me, Eunice, and the big payoff, but I got to set things up. I know a place where I can get phony I.D.'s and passports for the both of us. It'll take a few days, that's what the five grand's for."

"I guess you do have it all figured out." She smiled.

"You bet. Now speaking of baggage, how about helping me pack up?" He turned and started toward the bedroom.

"Mase . . ." Eunice stuck the spoon in the

yogurt carton and set the carton on the table.

"Yeah?"

She walked toward him and turned on the heat. She swayed that dancer's sway and let the kimono slip from her body onto the floor. She put her arms around him slowly. Her body was warm with anticipation and her lips cool from the yogurt. She pressed against his body and mouth.

"Mase, you have to go . . . right away?"

"Not . . . RIGHT away." He picked her up and carried her feet first into the bedroom.

It must have played something like that, and while Mase was hitting on Eunice I was awakened by somebody hitting on my door. My new door. The fact that I was on the couch sleeping, or trying to, didn't disturb them at all. They went right on banging, both workmen.

I rubbed the sleep out of my eyes and swam upstream to my feet.

"Good morning," I greeted the laborers, even through the sun had set.

They didn't miss a beat. I might as well have been invisible and deaf and dumb. These two were either devoted to their work, or they were snobs. I didn't much care; I went to the phone and put the receiver back onto its rightful resting place.

"You were out all afternoon," came a voice from the doorway. The voice didn't belong to either of the workmen. They were either tenors or baritones, I'd imagine. This was an alto. The voice and body belonged to Goldie Rose.

"I'm still out," I said. "Come in, come in, that's what new doors are for."

She walked between the two workmen who kept right on banging and screwing.

"Pleasant dreams?" She smiled and pointed toward the couch.

"You don't want to know," I intoned and smiled as suggestive a smile as I could muster.

"Maybe I do." Her suggestive tone and smile topped mine by a mile.

I lit a Lucky.

She walked to the typewriter and looked at the page.

"Writer's block?"

"On page one," I nodded. "Paragraph one."

"Still, not a bad beginning. You know what James Joyce said."

"No. What did James Joyce say?"

"He said that 'all fiction is fantasized autobiography.' "

"That helps."

"Would some dinner help? I'm one hell of a cook."

"I'll bet you are. But tonight I'm going to try to get a date with a cop."

"Oohh-kaayy."

"No, I'm serious. But dinner tomorrow night. I'll take you someplace nice — and I'd like you to meet my mother."

"Don't get that serious."

"I mean she's Greek."

"So was Aphrodite." Elliot was standing at the door as one of the workmen screwed on the nameplate. "I hope I'm interrupting a love tryst."

"You aren't," said Goldie.

"Pity."

"Alex just turned me down for a cop."

"For once," said Elliot, "I decline to comment."

"That is a kindness," commented Morgan Noble as she appeared at the doorway, "you should bestow on the world more often."

"I see that besides burglary," Elliot shot back, "you have added eavesdropping to your offenses."

"I was just on my way out, Elliott."

"Don't let us detain you for an instant."

"I thought I'd stop by and see how our hero is recuperating."

"Horseshit, Morgan. You don't give a fig for anybody but yourself. You have a heart, small and hard as an olive pit. I've had the misfortune to scan your self-serving banalities, which you borrowed so badly from Ayn Rand."

"At least I'm not some limousine liberal who . . ."

"Why don't you two hire a hall and charge admission?" Wes Weston's voice and body entered the conversation and doorway. "I'll take tickets."

"Better yet," Goldie smiled, "collaborate on a screenplay. Some of the best movies were made by people who hated each other; look at Raymond Chandler and Billy Wilder."

"I would prefer to die first," said Elliot, "a slow and agonizing death."

"I'll gladly provide the poison," Morgan said.

"Well, good people," Goldie started toward the door, "now that we know that Mr. Night is alive and well, I suggest that we go about our business and let him go about his."

At that the writers started to disperse, much to my relief.

"Don't forget," I touched Goldie's arm as she passed, "we've got a date tomorrow night. Think of something you'd like to do."

"Thanks, I consider that fair warning."

"Good work, gentlemen." Elliot paused, appraised the new door and spoke to the workmen. "First rate."

The workmen did not bother to respond. In fact they just left and so did everybody else. I walked to the phone to call Garter, but before I touched it, the phone rang.

"Hello, Alex."

"Hi, Mom."

"Just checking in. Did you have a nice day so far?"

Nice day?! Every bone and muscle in my body was complaining about the way I'd been treating it lately. There was still a buzz saw in my brain and it hurt to breathe. "Yeah, Mom, very nice day — so far."

"Pretty soft, being a writer these days, instead of a detective. Aren't you glad you took your mother's advice? Was I right or what?"

"You were right, Mom. You were absolutely right this time . . ."

"What do you mean by that?"

"By what?"

"By that 'this time' — like it was the first time, or the second, or the third. Is it a rare occasion when your mother is right about something?"

"That's not what I meant. I'm sorry, it just came out . . ."

"It's okay, Alex, I know what you mean, only teasing a little to see if I can still get a rise out of you."

"You can."

"I know it, but listen Alex, in this new soft profession you're in — don't let yourself get too soft. Keep going to the gym and working out, you hear me?"

"I went to the gym today, Mom, and I got a very good workout, believe me." Thanks to Bull Connors, I was going to add, but didn't.

"Are you and Myron still having dinner?"

"I was just going to call him."

"Did I tell you I was worried about him ever since his divorce? The real estate man was lucky Myron didn't shoot him. Like I said, he's put on a lot of weight since then . . ."

"The real estate man?"

"No! Myron. I think he's frustrated."

"Who isn't?"

"Man was not meant to live alone."

"Right."

"Both of you ought to get married."

"To each other?"

"Alex, don't talk that way in front of your mother."

"Sorry."

"Did you finish . . ."

". . . the book yet?" We both said that together.

"Not yet, Mom." Me, alone.

"Well, as Scarlett O'Hara used to say, 'Tomorrow is another day.' "

"Can't argue with that."

"Well, I'll let you go now, Alex. Want to come over tomorrow for dinner?"

"Not tomorrow, Mom. Got a date."

"Not with another actress, I hope."

"No, this is a good girl, Mom. I'll bring her by sometime."

"It's about time you got married and I'm right about that too!"

"I know you are. Goodnight, Mom."

"Goodnight, son."

We both hung up. I picked up the phone again and dialed Lieutenant Myron Garter's direct number.

Chapter Twenty-One

It wasn't easy but I finally convinced Garter to go along.

Over the phone I filled Myron in about Eunice and Mase, just enough to pique his policeman's curiosity. He said that I should call Lieutenant Wax. I promised to do that after he and I stopped by the Burke residence. Maybe Mase would provide us with incentive to book him and put him on ice for Wax. Wax could still make the collar for the murder. Wax would do the same for Garter.

Reluctantly, Garter agreed to the visit. But he said he had about an hour's work to finish up at the station. That was all right with me. I needed to go home to shower and gargle. I did.

An hour and fifteen minutes later Myron and I were on our way toward Genesee in his unmarked police car, just in case we brought back a passenger named Frank Mason, sometimes known as "Sport."

Neither of us brought up the subject of that morning's unpleasantness on the phone. It was just like old times and old friends, except that I knew something was still bothering him. Old friends can tell.

"What do you think of Goldie?" I idly inquired.

"Goldie Hawn? She's okay. Why do you ask?"

"Very funny. I mean Goldie Rose, the writer across the hall, and you know it."

"Oh that Goldie. Best looking writer I ever saw. Why? You got designs on her?"

"Depends on what you mean by 'designs.' "

"I think Webster defines 'design' as a 'plan, a project. A reasoned purpose, intention.' What are your intentions, Mr. Night?"

"Who knows? Maybe to settle down with her — and a good book, raise some short stories . . ."

"You?"

"Why not? I've changed professions; maybe it's about time I changed some other things."

"Yeah, why not? Except if you've changed professions, what the hell are we doing chasing after murderers?"

"Just cleaning up some unfinished business. There's Genesee."

"I see it."

★ ★ ★

Lieutenant Garter's knuckles knocked on the door marked "2G." Again, harder.

"Who is it?" Eunice's voice came from inside.

"Pizza man," I whispered.

"Police!" Garter gave me a dirty look and continued in his "official" voice. "Open up!"

"You got a warrant?" Eunice's voice was closer.

"You bet," Garter barked.

The door opened a couple of inches. Garter stepped forward to make sure it wouldn't close.

"Where is it?" Eunice asked.

"Where's what?" Garter answered.

"The warrant."

"On file." Garter pushed his way inside. I followed; Eunice was not pleased when she recognized me.

"You again," she grunted.

"Have you missed me?"

"Like I'd miss my hemorrhoids."

Eunice was wearing the same negligee as before. I wondered if she had any street clothes at all, but didn't comment. Garter and I both looked around. Myron had his gun in his hand just in case. Mine was still in its holster.

"Put away that goddamn gun, you sonofabitch."

"Where is he?" Myron inquired.

"Where's who?"

"Your boyfriend, Mason."

"He's not my boyfriend."

"Oh," I said, "he just drops by to use the shower." I unsheathed my .38 and went into the bathroom but I could still hear the conversation.

"Where is he?" Myron repeated.

"Where's who?" she repeated.

"The guy who's not your boyfriend."

The bathroom was empty except for a couple of dirty towels and another negligee on the tile floor. If Mase had brought over any toiletries — toothbrush, toothpaste, and shaving gear, they went with him when he left. But I thought I'd check the bedroom anyhow.

"He said he was leaving town," Eunice said.

"Where'd he say he was going?" Garter continued the interrogation, such as it was.

"Didn't say."

"And you're just waiting for a postcard — that it?"

"That's it, and you got no cause to come bustin' in here — hey, how do I even know if you're a cop?"

"You want to see my badge?"

"Stick it up your ass."

"Yes, Ma'am."

I came out of the bathroom and headed into the bedroom and turned on the light. It was just about what you'd expect — in a pig pen. I checked it out without touching anything I didn't have to. Garter was going on with his investigation.

"Know anything about an attempted jewel heist on New Year's Eve?"

"You already know what I know."

"What's that?"

"I know my stupid husband's dead."

"Try not to break down. Where were you then?"

"Right here."

"Alone?"

"No."

"Who with?"

"With Frank Mason."

"Just the two of you?"

"Right."

"Cozy."

"My husband and I are separated."

"Permanently," I said, as I came back into the parlor.

"Get any kicks while you were in there?" Eunice pointed into the bedroom and pointedly let her negligee flop open.

"Not as many kicks as Frank Mason, I'll wager."

"You couldn't hold a candle to him, droopdick."

"It didn't take Mason long to move in," Myron said.

"Life goes on," she sneered.

"How'd you like to spend the rest of your life in jail?" Garter sneered back.

"What for?"

"Accessory to murder — when the rap gets pinned on Mason. Think that over, Mrs. Burke."

"I will, after you two shitheads get out of here."

"You better think smart, if you want to stay out of jail. I'll bet the girls at CIW would just eat you alive."

"Blow!"

We did.

Chapter Twenty-Two

Without conversation we walked back to Garter's police car. It was a recycled former black and white Chevy Caprice, now all black.

"You hungry?" Garter asked, as he started up the engine. Before I could answer, the police radio also started up.

"25 David, 25 David," came the voice over the squawker, "1021 Station Watch Commander. 25 David — 1021 Station Watch Commander."

I knew it was for Garter — 25 David. His badge number is 425 — they use the last two digits. David is for Detective. 1021 means respond. Garter did.

"What's the message, Fred?"

"Call me back, 25 David. Important."

The squawker went dead.

"Goddamn it!" Myron seldom loses his cool. This was the second time today. He got the Watch Commander on the cellular.

"All right, Fred. What the hell is it?"

"It's your wife, lieutenant. Accident, I

guess. She's at Cedars Emergency . . ."

"What kind of accident?"

"O.D. Pretty bad, I'm afraid. Doctor said to get you over there . . ."

"Fred, don't shit me. Is she alive?"

"She was five minutes ago . . ."

Garter hung up and gunned the Chevy toward Cedars.

Five minutes later the Chevy was parked outside and we were in the Emergency Waiting Room talking to a nurse.

Yes. Rhoda was still alive but the chances of her making it were fifty-fifty. From the look on the nurse's face I doubted if the chances were that good.

No, Myron could not go in. They were still working on her. All he could do was wait. They'd let him know as soon as possible. He could see her then. The nurse didn't say "dead or alive" but that's what she meant.

We waited.

"I'm out of stogies," Myron said as we sat. "Let me have a cigarette. Will you, Alex?"

I had never seen Myron Garter smoke a cigarette before. But then again I had never seen tears in his eyes before either.

He inhaled deeply, then wiped at his face.

"Funny," he said, "I can smoke cigars all day long, but the minute I light up a cigarette the damn smoke curls right up into my eyes. Isn't that something?"

"Yeah."

"Alex, I got to tell you something . . ."

"Sure."

"What happened to Rhoda . . . it's my fault . . ."

"Myron . . ."

"No listen. I saw her last night. We had dinner together."

That explained a lot of things. Why he said he was going back to the station last night, why he got sore when I cracked wise this morning.

"Alex, you were there when she called yesterday afternoon. I swore I'd never see her again after what she . . . what happened. But I never heard her like that before. There was something about her, something . . . desperate. She promised she'd never bother me again if I'd see her just one time. So I said okay, I'd meet her.

"Jesus Christ, Alex, I barely recognized her — my own wife for eighteen years — and I barely recognized her. If I'd have passed her on the street I probably wouldn't have known her. You think I'm fat? She must have put on over a hundred pounds.

You remember how slim and beautiful she was. Well she isn't beautiful anymore either.

"I could hardly look at her and she knew it. I could tell she had her hair done and got all made up, but she looked terrible.

"She started crying and told me how sorry she was, said she'd do anything — all that crap about what a good man I was and she didn't deserve me — but she'd do anything if we could get back together — if we could just try.

"All the time she was crying and talking all I could do was think of that day when I found her and that sonofabitch in bed together, my bed, our bed, with him and his naked ass on top of her. How I never killed them both that day I'll never know — killed them and myself — well I didn't. But something else died. And the dead can't come back to life. They just can't.

"She kept on talking and I kept on thinking about that day and how many times it must've happened before even though she swore it never did.

"But it happened since, 'til he left her, the sonofabitch, for some young dame in the office. She went to hell, Alex, straight to hell after that. You know Rhoda, she never could drink, so she started eating, I guess.

Just like I did only a lot worse. Popping pills. Pills to lose weight. Pills to sleep. Pills! Pills! Pills! Morning, noon and night. She's a wreck. A bloated wreck.

"I sat there and listened to her spill her guts out and I didn't do or say a damn thing to help her. I can't excuse what she did and neither can she. But I wasn't any prize package as a husband either. All those years after we lost the baby, I was hardly ever home. I was a big hero with the department. I was a one-man band. Stick a broom in my ass and I'd clean up the joint. And I was also a real shitheel as a husband.

"The point is that, no matter what happened before, I didn't do or say one word last night that could have helped that woman in there. I just sat there and let her humiliate herself, whip herself to pieces, maybe to death — and I sat there holier than God Almighty and let her do it.

"If I had just given her one word of encouragement, one glimmer of hope . . . but I didn't. I let her fall apart. So there she is in there, maybe dead for all I know, and here I am — me — the one who called my best friend an asshole, when I'm the biggest, dumbest asshole in the world . . . let me have another cigarette, will you, Alex . . ."

"Sure."

But the door opened and a young Korean or Philippine doctor came in from the emergency room.

"Doctor . . ."

"Are you the husband, sir?"

"Yes, well . . . I'm Myron Garter . . . we're not . . ."

"You'd better come in."

"How is . . . is she alive?"

"Please follow me, sir."

I didn't know it at the time, but while we were in the hospital, across town another patch was being sewn into the quilt. Probably something like this:

In a semi-industrial area, there was a sign that identified a three-story brick building.

FEDONA
Wholesale jewelry
Imports — Exports

The building was mostly dark. But not entirely. Inside a dimly lit hallway Frank Mason followed Mike Fedona toward an office. Fedona was not quite as sturdy as Mason, but sturdy enough. He moved with an athletic gait and wore a well-tailored blue pinstripe double-breasted suit the same size as his age — forty-four.

"Is your partner here?" Mason asked.

Fedona opened the office door with his name painted on it and motioned for Mason to enter. Mason did and Fedona followed, still not answering the question.

The office was not quite as well tailored as Fedona's suit, but then a wholesaler doesn't want to put up too much of a front. He doesn't want his customers to get the idea that he's making too much of a profit from their business transactions.

"He's here," Fedona said finally. "Just as you requested."

"Good."

Colin Alderdyce sat in a leather chair near Fedona's desk. Fedona went to his chair behind his desk and sat. Nobody bothered to ask Mason to sit.

"Look here, Mason," Colin said, "what the hell's all this about?"

"Take it easy, Colin," Fedona smiled his businessman smile. "That's what we're all here to find out."

"Right," said Mason, not smiling. "First of all did you bring it?"

Colin pulled a bulging envelope from inside his breast pocket and whacked it against the top of the desk.

"Good," Mason finally smiled. "Let's have it."

"Just a minute," Colin held onto the envelope. "Let's get a few things straight first."

"Like what?"

"Like what happened in that hospital in Palm Desert. Goddamn it, Mason, killing Burke wasn't part of the deal . . ."

"Neither was Night's trying to kill us. He damn near did. Why the hell didn't you hire some patsy? Somebody who wouldn't try to play hero? Somebody who would've just turned the stuff over to us? Then Burke would still be alive and the deal wouldn't have gone sour."

"Don't you ever listen? I told you that Night's been driving her to the party for three years. It would have looked phony to hire somebody else. Besides she wouldn't have done it. She likes Night, treats him . . . well, like her own son. You should have knocked him out."

"I TRIED. He don't knock so easy. I hit him with everything I had. He must have a dome like an iron ball."

"You knew he had a gun."

"I thought he was out of it. What's done is done!"

"Including Burke."

"Why don't you just shut up, Alderdyce. I'm the one who took the chance. Burke was all right so long as things were going smooth. But he was a real nut case. He would've cracked and sent us all up."

"Maybe he would have died anyhow."

"And maybe not. That was my only shot to get him and I took it. After that it would've been too late. Goddamnit Alderdyce, you're not dealing with some amateur. I know what I'm doing!"

"So does Night. He's no amateur either."

"Gentlemen," Fedona spoke in an even tone still playing the peacemaker. "There's no point in fighting among ourselves. But Mase, Colin's right about Night. First of all it was a mistake for you to take up with . . . that lady so soon."

"Look, don't butt into my private life. Maybe it was, but I thought the heat was off."

"Evidently it isn't," Fedona still spoke calmly. "Not if Night keeps coming around."

"So what if he did come around? He never saw my face. Besides, I got an alibi. I was with Eunice that night. She'll swear to it."

"Some alibi," Colin commented.

"Just shut up about her and gimme the envelope."

Colin handed Mason the envelope and looked at Fedona.

"Five grand?" Mason looked inside.

"Count it," Colin said.

"I trust you, and you have to trust me. That's how it is with partners."

"This dissolves our partnership, Mr. Mason," said Colin. "Let's have that understood. I'll get my mother to call off Alex Night."

"Night's not gonna do a thing," Mason said. "I promise."

"Just a minute, Mason." Fedona still maintained his composure but his voice took on a slight edge. "What do you think you're going to do?"

"Me?" Mason put the envelope into his breast pocket. "I'm going to leave town — leave the country. Nobody'll ever see me again . . ."

Colin and Fedona looked at each other as if they had passed a milestone, but it turned into a millstone.

". . . as soon as I get the final payment — by the end of this week. That's how long it'll take to settle my affairs."

"What final payment?" Colin stood up.

"The final payment of fifty grand you're going to give me."

"You're crazy!" Colin sputtered and looked toward Fedona. "Mike, he's crazy!"

"Am I? Fellas, be reasonable. You don't

expect me to start a new life and enjoy a honeymoon on birdseed." He patted the envelope in his pocket. "This is just seed money."

"Mason," said Fedona, "don't try that. You're in this as deep as we are — deeper. Much deeper."

"Oh, no I'm not. If we hang, we all hang together, except out here it's injection."

"Killing Burke was your idea," Colin stammered. "We had nothing to do with it."

"That's not the way I'll tell it, and they'll believe me. I'm just a poor dumb slob who did what he was told to do. I was taken advantage of by a couple of rich, greedy bastards. I don't think there'll be many rich greedy bastards on the jury. They'll love it."

"Where the hell do you think I'm going to get fifty thousand dollars?"

"Oh you'll get it, Mr. Alderdyce. Your kind has ways of getting things."

"I can't possibly . . ."

"Sure you can. Consider it a gambling debt. You gambled and lost. I'll be in touch." Mason walked toward the door, paused and turned back. "Goodnight . . . partners."

That's about how it must have gone while I waited for Myron Garter to come out of the emergency room. It seemed like hours, but when I looked at my Elgin I realized that it had only been six or seven minutes. Still it was too long. But then I thought to myself, the longer the better. The doctor wouldn't let him stay in there all that time with a dead woman. I felt better.

So did Myron when he came out. He was almost smiling.

He just stood there for a couple of seconds, then he nodded. I went up to him, pumped his hand and whacked him on the shoulder.

"It was close, Alex. Too damn close. She swallowed every pill ever invented. I guess she's taken so damn many of them she built up a resistance. Would've killed anybody else."

"Maybe she just wanted to live, Myron. Just to see that ugly kisser of yours."

He shrugged.

"You hungry?" I asked. "We haven't had anything to eat."

"No, I don't think so . . . I think I'll just drop you off, go home . . . and . . ."

"Yeah, let's do that, pal."

Chapter Twenty-Three

The next morning I called Lieutenant Louis Wax in Palm Desert and filled him in on my visit to the demure widow Burke and the presence of one Frank Mason who I made out to also be Bogus number one. I also made sure not to bring Garter into the picture.

Wax asked, reasonably enough, if I could positively identify Mason since Bogus number one wore a ski mask during our little adventure. I said that I could positively identify him, but not absolutely positively. I also tossed the "Sport" dialogue into the pot.

Wax was only mildly impressed with my investigative acumen. He too had paid a visit to Mrs. Negligee who had made it a point to mention the fact that on New Year's Eve and into the next morning she was at home and in the company of one Frank Mason, which would blow my tenuous identification of the masked man out of the water — and out of court — unless he, or I, or somebody else came up with something better.

"Like fingerprints?" I asked.

"Like fingerprints," he answered.

"Well did you find any? On the wrecked car or at the hospital that would tie him into it?"

"Clean," was Wax's laconic response.

"Yeah," I said. "I did hear that they've invented gloves. Come to think of it, they were both wearing them that night."

"So they were," Wax added. "So they were. But we've got an APB out on Mason anyhow to question him. He might crack."

"And he might not. From what I've seen I bet on 'not.' "

"Thanks for the call," Wax said, so I figured that that was just about the end of our conversation. But I had done my duty, anyhow. I gave him my new office number and bade him good-bye and good luck.

On my way to the office I stopped by The Mysterious Book Store on Beverly Boulevard — 8763 Beverly Boulevard to be exact. Sheldon MacArthur, the manager, had left a message on my answering machine at home saying that he located a Pocket Book edition of Raymond Chandler's *Trouble Is My Business*, a collection of four short stories. "Trouble Is My Business," "Fingerman," "Goldfish" and "Redwind." I had wanted to add the volume to my Chandler collection.

Over the last few years, since Mysterious opened in Los Angeles, Sheldon and I had gotten to be pretty good chums. I even knew him before that, when he worked at B. Dalton Pickwick for Louis Epstein, the dean of all bookstore operators. Sheldon is a corduroy kind of fellow, about five and a half feet off the ground with steel rimmed spectacles, sandy hair and a bushy mustache to match. The store is owned by Otto Penzler in New York, whose name — come to think of it — is much like Dr. Otto Penzer's in Palm Desert.

The Mysterious Book Store has about fifteen thousand square feet of space with walls climbing up to twelve-foot ceilings all lined with books. Over one hundred thousand of them, hardcover and paperback, new and used, and mostly mysteries.

I used to stop by there when I was in the detective business, mostly on Sundays, when famous authors would be there signing their books. Donald Westlake, Eric Wright, James Ellroy, P. D. James, Sue Grafton, Elmore Leonard, Robert Parker and Julie Smith. (Julie Smith is the prettiest, not the best, only one of the best, but definitely the prettiest.) I've got most of their stuff and most of them signed by the authors.

When I first got the idea of switching to the writing racket, I could just picture myself there on some Sunday afternoon, sitting at one of those two wooden tables autographing stacks of my latest Edgar Award–winning novel that had been on the best seller list for months and was now being made into a motion picture starring Kevin Costner, Robin Williams and Michelle Pfeiffer, with the author making a cameo appearance.

All I had to do was fill in three hundred blank pages with plot twists and terse dialogue. Given enough time a monkey could do it.

I charged the Pocket Book edition of *Trouble Is My Business* to my Visa card (twenty-five bucks) and proceeded to drive west on Beverly Boulevard toward the WRITERS AND ARTISTS BUILDING.

When I got there, instead of going straight into my office I knocked on the door marked "G. Rose."

"Good morning," she said when Goldie opened the door.

"Good morning." I smiled. "What time?"

"About eleven," she said, looking at her wristwatch.

"Isn't that a little late to go on a date?"

"Oh, that. I thought you meant what time is it now. How's seven-thirty?"

"Seven-thirty is better."

"Come on in," she beckoned.

"Aren't you writing?"

"No, I'm just plotting. Come on in." I did.

"How's the bruised bod?"

"Black and blue and yearning for you."

"Poetry."

"Truth."

"Sit down."

"You sure?"

"Sit."

"Thanks." I made it onto the straight-back chair she had allowed for occasional visitors. "Matter of fact, I did want to ask you about something you said yesterday but it can wait 'til tonight. That way we can have something to talk about."

"We'll find something to talk about to-night, I'm sure. What was it?"

"You said that Chandler and Wilder hated each other when they were working on the *Double Indemnity* script . . ."

"That's right . . ."

"Happens to be one of my favorite

books and pictures . . . ."

"Mine too."

"Why?"

"Why what?"

"Why did they hate each other?"

"Two different types," she shrugged and sat in her chair. I tried not to look at her legs, but not hard. "Two different worlds. Billy spoke broken English with a comical German accent and it's not easy to be German and comical, but he was. Always had to have a collaborator because of the language barrier. A cocky, jaunty little guy. Chandler, as you know was just the opposite."

"Yeah I know. Educated in England. Formal, staid, you might say, drunk or sober."

"Mostly drunk."

"Right. Still, drunk or sober, he had a condescending attitude toward the funny little foreigner. He didn't much like Cain either, or his novel, but he needed the money so he took the job."

"I'm glad he did."

"So am I, but he wasn't. They spent six months together in the same room. Chandler sucking on his pipe, filling the place with smoke, and hitting the bottle while Wilder strutted around like a comic opera dictator trying to disperse the smoke with a swagger stick, pointing it at Chandler and banging it on the furniture to drive home a point when they disagreed . . . which was incessantly."

"I reckon that would make for incompatibility."

"I reckon. Finally Chandler quit and went home and got even drunker. Wilder and Paramount begged him to come back, his stuff was that good."

"So he came back."

"Not until he had drawn up a list of complaints against Herr Wilder and demanded an apology and a signed statement that Billy would forego the swagger stick and treat him with due respect and also not wear his customary baseball cap while they were working."

"Sounds reasonable, up to the baseball cap. Did Wilder sign and comply?"

"On all counts. Until they finished the script, then Wilder went on swaggering and Chandler went on drinking, but they made a hell of a picture."

"Maybe there's hope for Elliott and Morgan."

"I don't think so."

"Neither do I. Well," I got up and went for the door, "thanks for the lesson . . ."

"I see you've been to Mysterious." She pointed to The Mysterious Book Store bag I was holding in my hand.

"Right."

"What have you got there, something new?"

"Something old. Speaking of Raymond Chandler, I picked up a Pocket Edition of *Trouble Is My Business*."

"Not his best work."

"Maybe he wasn't drunk enough when he wrote it."

"Maybe he was too drunk."

"Maybe."

"How's Sheldon?"

"Sober. See you tonight. Where do you want to eat?"

"At home. I'll make salad, spaghetti and sherbet."

That threw me for a couple of seconds, but I recovered nicely.

Chapter Twenty-Four

When I got in my office I called Myron Garter to find out how Rhoda was doing.

"She's doing okay, Alex. I stopped by this morning. She looks a hell of a lot better. But they're going to keep her there for a couple of days."

"Good. How you feeling Myron? Get any sleep?"

"Yeah, I slept some, feel okay, but listen, Alex, I don't think I can have dinner with you tonight. I told Rhoda I'd stop by and — well, I just think she could use some company. Is that okay?"

"Sure, Myron. We'll do it some other time. Take care of yourself. Tell Rhoda I say hello. Talk to you later. By the way I talked to Wax, he's getting an APB out on Mason."

"Yeah we got it."

"So long."

"So long, Alex, and thanks."

That was a relief. In my grand design for, or on, Goldie and our date tonight I'd forgotten all about Myron. But it all worked out okay, better than the three of us going on the town — or on the couch.

Five seconds after I hung up, the phone rang.

"Hello."

"Hello, Alex? Is this Alex Night?"

"It is. Who's this?"

"Well hello, Alex, Hugh Brent here. How are you?"

His name was no more "Brent" than mine was "Night." I didn't like him. Not because he changed his name. Hell, even Marion Morrison did that. I didn't like him because he was a sleaze in a two-thousand-dollar suit. And even more of a sleaze out of his two-thousand-dollar suit. The word "pervert" was invented in his honor — or dishonor. He worked as an executive for a major studio. It doesn't matter which one.

I had done a job for him once and had to hold my nose for a week, even in the shower. The job involved getting back some pictures when he wasn't wearing a two-thousand-dollar suit.

"I'm okay, Mr. Brent . . ."

"Please, Alex, call me Hugh, we go back a hundred years."

It was actually five or six years, but I didn't want to go back at all — or forward.

"What is it, Mr. Brent?"

"Well, it seems I'm in a bit of a pickle again . . ."

Yeah, I'll just bet, I thought to myself.

". . . It's difficult to explain over the phone, I'd like you to come by and . . ."

"Mr. Brent, didn't you hear? I'm out of the detective business . . ."

"Yes I did hear that, but I thought you might want to just help out in this case . . ."

"Why would I want to do that?"

"Well frankly," his voice became more frank and less friendly. "It would take very little time and effort on your part and it would be worth five thousand dollars to me . . ."

"Not to me, it wouldn't."

"Well, couldn't we just talk about . . ."

"We already have — and I'm about to say good-bye."

"Perhaps you could recommend another P.I.?"

"I could recommend a psychiatrist, but I'm not going to."

So I hung up.

I'm no saint, but those kind of guys make me sick. Cruel, bestial little bastards who revel in degrading and dehumanizing vulnerable people — men and women and children — then come sniveling around with a checkbook to bail themselves out so they can revert to their perversions until they get caught again or until somebody slices out their tongue and sticks it where the sun never shines.

The phone rang again. That bastard just doesn't give up, I thought to myself and picked up the receiver and barked.

"HELLO! . . ."

"Alex, this is Cynthia Alderdyce."

I was glad that I hadn't barked for Hugh Brent to go do something unnatural.

"Hello, Mrs. A.," I said nicely, nicely.

"How is the new master of mystery?"

"I don't think the old masters have anything to worry about."

"Now don't be modest."

"In my case, it becomes me."

"How's the leg?"

My, my, I thought, we're unusually full of small talk today, but held back. "It's fine Mrs. A., thanks again for getting that check from AmBrit."

"A mere trifle."

"Not to me. It makes for a pretty good poke when you're starting out in a new business."

"Alex, are you making any progress on that matter we spoke of?"

"Some. Thanks mostly to Myron Garter. I've got a sheet on him — name was Burke.

James Wesley Burke. And don't worry, Mrs. A., he didn't have any family except for a wife and they were split."

I didn't mention that what split them was a jackhammer named Mason who favored Magnums and most likely tossed Senor Burke off a roof to de-energize him.

"I see," Mrs. A. said after a slight pause. "Any word on his accomplice?"

"Matter of fact, I'm working on that." And that was the truth, or part of it.

"Alex, I don't want you to endanger yourself."

"Neither do I."

"It just isn't worth it. We have the jewels back; besides my main concern was for the man's family."

"Rest easy on that score, Mrs. A., the widow is already starting a new life."

"Well I'm glad to hear that."

"You want me to bring the sheet over?"

"No hurry. It so happens I'm having a little party on Friday night. Why don't you come by about eight and bring along the 'sheet' then. How does that sound?"

"It sounds elegant. Can I also bring along a lady friend?"

"Of course. Just keep her away from Colin. Bye, Alex."

"Bye."

If Colin Alderdyce so much as looked at Goldie I'd brain him with that Swedish meatball.

Well, well, well, Alex ol' top, I thought to myself, you're not doing so bad. Ten big ones in the bank, back in the good graces of Myron Garter, a date with Aphrodite tonight, in her chambers no less, and maybe you can talk her into that swellegant party on Friday. What more can you ask?

Then I looked at the typewriter. It stared back at me with that tongue of white paper sticking out of its roller.

I waited it out for a few minutes, thinking there would be some interruption. The phone would ring. It would be my mother. Or Myron Garter. Or some pervert. But the phone didn't ring.

I looked at the door, partly open. Maybe Goldie would stop by. Or Elliot. Or Morgan. The Bernstein brothers. Wes Weston. Even Bull Connors, loose again. But no. Nothing. There was just the typewriter and me, all alone in the room. In Beverly Hills. For all I knew, in the world.

Well, there was no reason to put it off any longer.

Yes, there was. Research!

You can't just sit down and write a book. I

learned that the hard way. You've got to do research.

I reached for the Pocket Book Edition of Raymond Chandler's *Trouble Is My Business*, went to the Naugahyde couch, lay there, and began to read twenty-five dollars worth.

"Anna Halsey was about two hundred and forty pounds of middle-aged putty-faced woman in a tailor-made suit. Her eyes were shiny-black shoe buttons, her cheeks were as soft as suet and about the same color . . ."

What I didn't know was that while I was making and receiving telephone calls from my office, another telephone conversation was taking place between a couple of other players involved in our little drama. From what I later pieced together, part of the dialogue between Eunice Burke and Frank Mason must have gone about like this:

". . . so you didn't leave none too soon, Mase."

"You sure that other guy was a cop?"

"That's what he said. He sure as hell looked and acted like a cop. A fat cop."

"You didn't ask to see any I.D.?"

"No, nor tattoos either. I'm telling you, Mase, I know a cop when I smell one. How did it go with Fedona?"

"It went just like I said it would."

"Did you get the dough?"

"Let's say I got the down payment, five grand. It'll take them a few days to raise the rest . . ."

"How much is the rest?"

"Fifty."

"Fifty what?"

"Fifty grand, that's what."

"Jesus Christ, Mase! Fifty G's! There ain't that much money."

"There will be for the two of us. But I got to lay low and get those passports first."

"Why can't I lay low with you?"

"Because they could be tailing you. You got to wait 'til the last minute. I'll pick up the dough. They could spot the two of us a lot easier. And when you come to meet me be sure you lose them . . ."

"Don't worry, I know how. I'll be zigging and zagging . . ."

"Listen, don't pack anything. That'll be a tip-off. Just leave everything. Just come with the clothes on your back . . ."

"Do I get a whole new wardrobe?"

"You get a whole new everything, including me. Call me Saturday."

"Mase . . ."

"What?"

"Do you miss me?"

"Sure I miss you. But I'm not gonna miss Mr. Night. Him I'm gonna GET."

Chapter Twenty-Five

I never shaved so close, or smelled so good in all my life.

I had clipped my fingernails, my toenails, had taken a hot needle shower and slowly turned the knob to "cold" until my body was blue. I had inserted a new blade and scraped away all trace of hirsute on my happy face. I had splashed on the "Brut" with a lavish hand from forehead to both feet.

I was decked out in my one and only dark blue Chester Barrie sport coat and my finest pair of severely-creased pearl gray trousers. I was a sight right out of *Gentlemen's Quarterly*, which is now published every month. A well-mannered paisley tie added the perfect effect, set off against a blazing white, crisply starched Carroll and Company shirt.

I was irresistible.

So was Goldie Rose when she opened the door. She was a vision in varied hues of blue, from pale to sapphire to indigo. The blue orchid I brought along was just the right touch. And I touched her lightly as I pinned it on. Her hair was loosely spinning gold and it sent me spinning.

Goldie's condo was right out of a movie set and so was she. Not at all sparse and utilitarian like her office. It was warm and fluffy and fashioned for comfort, that's right, and so was she. She showed me around. What used to be the second bedroom she had converted into a den-library where it was evident she worked on her doctorate. Two walls were neatly jammed with books. On one wall, mystery and detective works, the usual ones, most of them I had also.

The other wall was stocked with books which I didn't have, and haven't read. I can only remember a few of the titles and maybe I haven't got them right: *Science and Human Behavior*; *Crime, Justice and Correction*; *Principles of Behavior Modification*; and *Psychotherapy by Reciprocal Inhibition*.

Then we walked through the rest of the place — except for her bedroom.

"Would you like to make us some cocktails?"

"I would, I certainly would," said I gallantly going for the bar. "You're a scotch person as I recall."

"Not at home."

"What is your preference at home?"

"Gin."

"Gin?! A grand choice. Happens to be mine too. It's been said that I make the most perfect martini since . . . Nick Charles."

"Go ahead, Nick. I'll be Nora."

This couldn't be happening, but it was.

"I hope you don't mind if I stir the spaghetti sauce while you stir the martinis, Nick. It's the maid's night off."

"Too bad. I like dear old Bridget. I'll miss her tonight." I mixed a couple of stiff ones.

"What kind of place do you live in, Nick?"

"It's a condo too, over on Wilshire and Fremont. Nothing like this. But you'd love it. Used to belong to a whore."

We tipped glasses.

"Yasso," we both said, which is the Greek equivalent of "Skol," or "good health."

"Are you serious about the whore?"

"On my honor."

"Sit here on the couch and tell me about . . ."

" 'It' or 'her'?"

"Both."

"Well, she was a whore," I said as we sat. "Her name was Gilda, a redhead and a client of mine it so happens . . ."

"Who was the client? You or she?"

"Dear lady, please. Do you want to hear the story or not?"

"I do."

"It appears she displeased one of her customers one stormy night so he proceeded to chop her up into little pieces and redecorate the walls with her blood."

"Oh, a bedtime story."

"Sort of. After that the condominium association had a devil of the time finding a buyer even after they redid the place with wood paneling to wipe away all trace of the former resident and her profession. Every time a prospective buyer appeared, somebody in the building let the proverbial cat out of the bag."

"How unfortunate."

"Not for me. I played the catbird game, waiting until the price went down, down, down — and then I pounced."

"Congratulations."

"Can you keep a secret?"

"No."

"No matter. It's too late for anybody to do anything about it anyhow."

"About the murderer?"

"Oh, no. He confessed and found sanctuary in San Quentin."

"Then what's the secret?"

"That 'somebody in the building who

let the proverbial cat out of the bag . . .' "

"No! Not you!"

"I feel better," I nodded, "now that I've confessed."

"How do you sleep in that room? Don't you ever dream of Gilda?"

"Who's Gilda?"

We had another magnificent martini and then ate. Make that dined. Goldie had tossed up a Greek salad in celebration of our mutual bloodlines. Tomatoes, onions, cucumbers, feta cheese and Calamata olives, with olive oil and vinegar dressing. She had concocted a sauce for the gods, the goose and the gander. Liberally sprinkled with oregano and several other spices with a flotilla of sausages floating around. The pasta was spagatina, and the wine was red, and the conversation was liberally sprinkled with laughter and innuendo.

As advertised, the desert was sherbet, combination orange, raspberry and pineapple, liberally sprinkled with Grand Marnier.

We both stacked the dishes after Goldie suggested that I remove my jacket, loosen the paisley and be more comfortable. I stripped to the degree she suggested.

She put on a King Cole tape — *The Nat King Cole Story* — and at her further suggestion we repaired to the sofa with the bottle of Grand Marnier and a pair of oversized snifters while the "King" serenaded the two of us.

After we "Yassoed" again and sipped, she pointed to the bottle.

"You like oranges?"

"If they're from your tree." I had read that somewhere.

"Well, go ahead," she said after smiling appropriately at my borrowed *bon-mot*.

"Go ahead," I repeated, "that's pretty damned dangerous on your part, 'go ahead' and what?"

"You promised to tell me why you quit being a private investigator."

"Oh that, well that's no great shakes of a story. The real detective business, unlike the stuff you and everybody else write about, isn't what's it's cracked up to be in fiction . . ."

"But I understand that you dealt mostly with people in show business, glamorous people . . ."

"There are no glamorous people, sister. There's just people. And nobody ever came to call unless he or she was in trouble."

"As Chandler wrote," she sipped and smiled, " 'trouble is my business.' "

"Yeah but usually it was pretty dull and

dreary and when it wasn't I got tired of carrying all that extra lead in my system. Would you like to see my etchings? They're all over my body."

"Some other time," she said. "Maybe when we go swimming this summer."

That was promising. King Cole was singing "Blue Gardenia" and I was studying the blue orchid on her breast.

"So now your ambition is to be a novelist."

"No. My ambition is to get you on my boat."

"You own a boat?"

"Not yet, but I'll get one, a slow boat — like the song says, we'll take a slow boat to China. How's that sound?"

"Oh, I don't know. I'm pretty particular. What's the name of your boat?"

"I'm not particular. You name it."

"I'll tell you what. A boat's got to have two sides. You name one side. I'll name the other."

"Fair enough. You take starboard, I'll take port. You first."

"Okay. *True Love*. That was Bing Crosby and Grace Kelly's boat in *High Society*."

"Right," I said. "And before that it was Cary Grant and Katharine Hepburn's in *The Philadelphia Story*."

"What's the name of your side?" she smiled.

"*Briny Marlin*."

"*Briny Marlin*? What's that mean?"

"It's from another Cary Grant picture, *Mr. Lucky*. It was set during WW II, and he played a draft dodging heel of a gambler with a Greek name, Joe Bascopolous, who had a gambling ship called *The Fortuna*, fell in love with a society girl played by Laraine Day. Their love, true love I guess, reformed him — so he re-named the ship *Briny Marlin* and risked his life taking a shipload of relief goods to Europe for Greece and the other Allies."

"But why *Briny Marlin*?"

"It's cockney rhyming slang — he used it all through the picture. 'Tit for tat' was 'hat,' 'storm and strife — wife,' 'fiddle and toot — suit,' 'lady from Bristol — pistol,' 'bottle and stopper — copper,' 'soft and fair — hair,' " I touched her hair. " 'Sparkle and prize — eyes,' " I touched her eyes. " 'I suppose — nose,' " I touched the tip of her nose. " 'North and south — mouth,' " I touched her mouth, but not with my hand. I leaned close and kissed her.

She didn't pull back. So I kissed her some more. Nat King Cole was singing "Nature Boy" and nature was beginning to take its course.

Finally she did pull back. I'd like to think reluctantly, but I let her. She looked at me and I looked at her, and nothing could be as it was before, not between us. I thought of all the other girls that I had kissed, and more. Never, never, never had I felt like this. I knew it and I think she knew it. I knew she knew it.

"What does Briny Marlin rhyme with?"

"Darlin'."

"I like the name of your boat."

"Want to take that trip to China?"

"Not yet, Alex."

Somehow, I knew she'd say that. I can't say that I wasn't disappointed. But I wasn't surprised. She just wasn't the kind to land in bed on the first bounce. But this time she kissed me. It was soft and tender and tasted of the sweetest oranges I had ever savored.

"Briny Marlin," I whispered, "I can't bear much more."

"I know. Me too. We better call it a night." She rose.

"Goldie," I got up and put my arms around her.

"Alex, let's give it a little time."

"You're the skipper, mate."

I put on my coat and walked to the door. She followed.

"Thanks," she kissed me again, but I

knew it was a goodnight kiss.

"Goodnight, Briny Marlin," I said.

When I left Nat King Cole was singing "To the Ends of the Earth." But I didn't want to go to the ends of the earth.

All I wanted was a slow boat to China.

Chapter Twenty-Six

I drove home and took a cold shower. I washed everything except my face. I wanted the taste of her sweet, red lips and the orange Marnier to linger all night.

I had just come back from a high school prom date. As the song says, I was just a kid again doing what I did again — which wasn't damn much. It boiled down — or up — to three kisses. For a man of the world, a veteran of a foreign war, a badge-carrying cop, a hot-shot private eye — that didn't exactly add up to a torrid love affair. It added up to three kisses.

The hell it did. Tonight was just a prelude and I knew it. This was the overture. I could feel a song coming on, with drums beating, horns blaring, trombones sliding and violins playing.

What did I care about jewel thieves and murderers, and merry widows? About pervert producers and punks like Petey Boyle?

At long last, love. I had found my Briny Marlin. I was Nick Charles, Sam Spade,

Philip Marlowe and Joe Bascopolous all rolled up in one. Cary Grant wasn't Mr. Lucky.

I was.

Hell, I was such a kid again I had forgotten two important things.

One, I forgot to smoke any cigarettes all night. First time that had happened in twenty years.

Two, I forgot to ask Goldie about going to Mrs. Alderdyce's swellegant party on Friday night. I could call her right now, I thought, but no, that would be anticlimactic, even though the evening didn't have a climax. I'd wait until morning, then pop into her office and ask her face to face.

And what a face. I could see her now, her lovely face and hair resting gently against a pillow in bed, in a bedroom I had never seen — yet.

Was she thinking of me? Sure she was. Goodnight, I said. Goodnight, Briny Marlin. And goodnight Gilda — where ever you are.

Chapter Twenty-Seven

Thursday morning I woke up when the phone rang. Well, I thought, somebody in this world gets up earlier than I do. Maybe it was Goldie.

It wasn't.

"Good morning, Alex."

"Good morning, Mom."

"Did I wake you?"

"Uh, no. I was just having a bowl of cereal."

"Good. Alex, what's this I hear about Rhoda?"

"I don't know, Mom. What do you hear?"

"Don't play games with your mother. I called Myron yesterday and he told me Rhoda took poison. I tried to call you last night but you were out on the town."

"I wasn't out on the town and she didn't take poison. It was pills."

"Pills, poison. She tried to kill herself."

"I guess so."

"Why would she do that?"

"I don't know. I haven't talked to her."

"Guilty conscience?"

"Maybe."

"I like Rhoda."

"That's good."

"In spite of what she did to Myron."

I made no comment.

"Are you there, Alex?"

"I'm here."

"Why don't you say something?"

"I don't know. Maybe because I had cereal in my mouth."

"Oh . . . well, what do you think?"

"About what?"

"What do you mean, 'About what?' About whether Myron and Rhoda will get together again. He said the real estate man left her."

"That's right. He did."

"Well, what do you think?"

"I don't know, Mom. I'll think it over."

"Well it's not up to you, you know."

"Yeah, I know."

"Alex."

"What?"

"Come over for dinner tonight."

"Well . . ."

"Never mind the well, just come over. I want to talk to you about something."

"Okay, Mom, I'll come over, but it might be a little late. I want to do some writing."

"Come over anytime, I'll keep the food hot."

"Okay."

"Have a nice day, Alex."

After assuring my mother that I would have a nice day I did have some cereal, my usual three cups of coffee made in my usual aluminum drip pot, which they don't make anymore, a slice of rye toast heaped with orange marmalade. The orange marmalade made me think of Goldie Rose, but then again I had been mostly thinking about Goldie Rose since last night.

I hit the Hollywood YMCA and had my usual workout while listening to the usual bullshit from the usual bunch of bullshitters who worked out there regularly.

There was the director, mostly TV, over sixty years old who still thought he was sixteen and still had the same butch haircut he had in high school and the Army, and played racquetball as if the honor of the regiment rested on his winning. He usually won.

There was the beefy actor whose mood varied with his unemployment status. But he could get an awful lot of conversation out of a couple days' work. A two-day job was good for two months' conversation. For a couple of weeks it was, "I'm going to do a

'Seventh Heaven.' " Then for a couple more weeks, "doing a 'Seventh Heaven.' " Then for a month or more, "just finished a 'Seventh Heaven.' "

There was the preacher. An encyclopedia salesman who had heard the voice and had seen the face of God, and who sold and proselytized door to door and in the steam room.

There was the real estate salesman, who, by the way he grimaced and gimped needed a hip replacement and as his condition deteriorated continued to declare that nature was healing the avascular necrosis, and the pain was subsiding. At that point I gave him another nine months before he went under the knife. Actually, under the saw.

There was another actor who had been on a successful television sitcom for six years and kept yearning to go back to the "theatre" in New York where his true talent could be appreciated, instead of exploited for a lousy half a million dollars a season.

There was the retired professor whose idea of exercising was to work the *Los Angeles Times*' daily crossword puzzle on the toilet, or in the steam room and upside down, while the blood dripped to his head in what I guess was some sort of yoga position.

There were the usual others who came and went. On one wall of the lounge area there were about a dozen plaques commemorating those who "went" in the last few years.

It was an honor devoutly not to be wished by me. Not for a long, long time. What I wished for was at the WRITERS AND ARTISTS BUILDING in Beverly Hills. That was my next stop.

I knocked on the door with "G. Rose" on the nameplate.

"Come in."

I did.

"Good morning, Briny Marlin."

"Good morning, yourself," she turned and smiled.

"Am I interrupting your strain of thought?"

"My train is right on track. How about yours?"

"De-railed, as usual."

"Discipline, my man, discipline."

"I thought I showed a good deal of discipline last night — and restraint."

"You were a perfect gentleman."

"I hope I don't live to regret it."

"Seriously, Alex, it was very nice."

"It was so nice that I forgot to ask you something. Thought about calling you after I left, but didn't."

"That's funny, I thought maybe you might. Matter of fact, I almost called you."

"What stopped you?"

"Discipline."

"Damn I'm getting to hate that word."

"What was it you forgot to ask?"

"I've been invited to a party tomorrow night. The party giver said I could come only if I brought along the most beautiful girl in Beverly Hills . . . so . . ."

"So . . . ?"

"So how'd you like to come along so they'll let me in?"

"Might be arranged. Are we dressing?"

"What kind of a party do you think I'd take you to?"

"I meant 'fancy-schmancy.' "

"I'd say 'semi-schmancy,' just to be safe."

"Somehow I thought you and 'safe' didn't mix."

"Unsubstantiated rumors and unmitigated lies. Will you come with me and be my love and we will all the pleasures prove . . ."

"Well, Mr. Marlowe — Christopher, not Philip — let's just say I'll come with you."

"That's a start. Maybe we can work up to a 'wow' finish."

"Maybe."

"Great! Going to quit while I'm ahead.

Meanwhile, if you need anything, just whistle. I'll be right across the hall. Going to write up a storm — or a murder."

"Discipline!"

"Damn right!"

I started to write. That's right, the phone rang.

"Hello."

"Good morning. Is this Mr. Night?"

"Yeah, who're you?"

"Mr. Night, this is Clara in Mr. Meadow's office. He's been trying to reach you all morning, will you please hold?"

Dear old Clara was good at it. She didn't give me a chance to answer. She had been with Meadows for years and knew how to handle all comers. Meadows was on the phone in less than four seconds. Mike Meadows was not the sort of man to waste words or time.

"Good morning, Alex. I need your help."

"Mike . . ."

"Alex, I'm in a jam and so is Frances . . ."

"What else is new?"

"She walked off the set . . ."

"She's walked off before. She'll walk back on."

"Not this time. I've got a whole damn company up in Carmel, a very expensive company; they're standing around with the meter running. You know what an idle cast and crew costs these days? A fortune!"

"Mike . . ."

"The director wants to replace her."

"Tell him 'no.' You're the boss . . ."

"Every boss has got a boss. I've got a board of directors — the money people in New York and Korea. There's six producers on the picture and the director. Nobody wanted her in the first place. I rammed her down their throats and now they want to spit her out."

"Why'd you shove her into it? She told me she didn't want to do it."

"She told everybody. Alex, you know me pretty good. We go back a ways. Not as far back as Frances and me. Even then I saw something there, something nobody else saw — or wanted to see. But it was there. You know she was the biggest thing in town back in those days. Well, I know that it's still there . . . I had this part tailored for her. Every scene, every word, every move! Goddamn it she wants to do it. But she's afraid. She's scared to death of being an actress instead of everybody's fantasy lover. That she could handle. Everybody in town thinks I was laying her. Well I'll tell you something. I never even touched her. Never. In spite of all her money, this town tossed her onto the ash heap. Well, I'll tell you something else. I was right then — and I'm right about this part. If she doesn't do it I'll survive, I always have. But she won't. This is it. Fade out. For her, Alex. Not for me. For her! That's the longest speech I ever made in my life."

"Pretty damn good speech, Mike."

"Maybe you owe me, and maybe you don't. I don't keep track. But will you do it for her?"

"Do what?"

"I told them up there that she'd be back in Carmel by tonight, or we'd get somebody else tomorrow morning and shoot her stuff over. I know she's home. The phone's off the hook, but she's there. If I showed up, she'd throw me out. She's on a binge. Go talk to her. I've got the studio jet standing by. Get her on that plane. Drunk or sober, get her on it. I'll pay you whatever you want out of my own pocket . . ."

"Never mind the pay. What makes you think she'll listen to me?"

"I know about you and her, yeah and about all the others. But the others can't, or won't, do a damn thing. Maybe you can. Will you try?"

"What makes you think she won't throw me out either?"

"You don't throw so easy. If she does, I'll replace her. Will you try?"

"Okay, Mike, I'll try."

"Thanks. That's all I can say, but I mean it."

I knew he did.

Chapter Twenty-Eight

It's changed, I thought, driving toward Malibu. The whole town's changed, but not as much as the business. I was glad that I was out of it, even if I didn't know what business I was in at the moment.

At least when you're a private investigator you've got a license that says you are. And a gun. There's no license that says you're a writer. All you've got is a typewriter or a word processor and what you've had published or put on the movie screen or the television set.

So far, all I had was a typewriter with a single sheet of paper stuck in it. And I mean "stuck."

I never knew the "old Hollywood" studio era, when Leo the Lion was king of the jungle. When MGM was Tiffany with "more stars than there are in heaven." When the avuncular Louis B. Mayer and his entourage polished up such luminaries as Garbo, Gable, Garson, Tracy, Garland, Rooney, Harlow, Hepburn and Turner. In those days you didn't have to mention the actors by both names. There was only one Gable, one Harlow, one Turner — and it wasn't Ted.

If any studio exemplified the decline and fall of the studio system it was MGM. It went from the steeple to the cellar. From the Louvre to the lavatory. From Grand Hotel to Motel Six.

By now many of its stars literally are in heaven — or hell — but not all. Cyd Charise is still kicking, not very high. Mickey Rooney is a fat old man doing revivals of revivals.

There are a few other alumni from the latter years still breathing in and breathing out: Donald O'Connor, doing dinner theater — unsinkable Debbie Reynolds, splitting her time between TV and Las Vegas — June Allyson, hawking diapers — Esther Williams, selling bathing suits instead of wearing them — Elizabeth Taylor, between marriages and professional engagements — Katharine Hepburn, the oldest and grandest surviving lioness of them all. Ironically there's one grand lady who wasn't among the grandest of the MGM stars, even though she was one of the best, who's hit the jackpot. First on Broadway, then on television.

Angela Lansbury, a.k.a. Jessica Fletcher. Her series *Murder, She Wrote* gave jobs to quite a few MGM alumni who were much bigger than she was on Leo's lot. Kathryn Grayson, Gloria De Haven, Van Johnson, Howard Keel, Margaret O'Brien, Jane Powell, Hurd Hatfield, Janet Leigh and more. The fortunes of jungle warfare.

Years ago, a misfortune hunter named Kerkorian bagged Leo the Lion, skinned the king and stripped his kingdom. MGM has been passed around more often than a Christmas fruitcake. Chased off its own domain. The lot is still there in Culver City. Millions upon millions have been spent improving stages and offices.

But when you pass by the old MGM lot now, the sign says something else.

And that says a lot about the business. A business I used to be a small part of during its twilight time.

But, what the hell, they're still making moving pictures, except now they're calling them films. Fewer and much more expensive, but they're still making them. Frances Vale was supposed to be working in one of them. At the moment, she wasn't.

She was in Malibu. So was I. I had just pulled into her driveway where I had pulled in quite a few times before, in the old days.

Her real estate went right to the ocean. But it was walled. Wooden walled. From her backyard you had to open a gate in the wall to get to the beach. Or from the beach to get back to the estate. Right then I wanted to get from the beach into the estate. I had already rung the front door *sans* response. Even tried it. Locked.

I knew my Fairest of the Rare was in there all right. Her Mercedes was in the garage and the sound of music, if you could call it that, was rending the precinct.

As I walked toward the rear of the estate someone who looked suspiciously like Johnny Carson stuck his head out of the second-story window from the adjoining residence.

"Tell that broad to turn that goddamn music down!"

"Yes, sir." I nodded politely.

About a shovel full of sand had seeped into my shoes by the time I got to the back gate which fronted the ocean. I slipped off both moccasins, one at a time, let the sand seep out and replaced each shoe on the proper hoof.

I knew it was a waste of effort but I banged against the gate. With all that noise inside she couldn't have heard a gunshot go off. If I had had my .38 Police Special with me a gunshot would have gone off.

I banged again, and again. Then I tried the knob. Glory! Glory! The door opened.

I stepped right in like a preacher going to the pulpit to address his flock.

The entire flock appeared to be in the Jacuzzi. Both of them. Franny and Friend. Having been in the same hot water several times myself, I surmised the flock was naked. Both of them. Franny was president of the anti–bathing suit society. By the by, the Friend was a male friend.

I ignored both human beings and walked to the machinery that housed the music maker. It was one of those newfangled devices that conceals one of those newfangled disks or whatever they call them. I pushed a lot of buttons and out it popped. I broke it in half and let both halves drop.

I turned and addressed my flock.

"Greetings."

They were both smoking joints with one hand and holding a drink in the other. The bottle of Stolichnaya and pitcher of orange juice rested on a tray within immediate reach of the Jacuzzi.

"I'll give you greetings," said Friend.

He rose up from the Jacuzzi. Friend was big. All over. He set his glass on a table and flipped the joint at my moccasins.

"Alex," Franny smiled. "This is Jason. Jason is a Black Belt."

"He seems to have left it at home," said I.

"I am home," said Jason. "And you're outta here!"

His voice was the only part of him that wasn't big. He sounded like a constipated canary.

"Nice voice," said I. "What do you eat? Birdseed? Or little boys?"

I think that got to him. He turned blue all over. And he trembled a little.

"You're gonna regret that," he peeped.

"Put on your skirt and blow, little girl."

He trembled even more. That's what I wanted. The madder he got, the better. But he didn't let me get him any madder. He came at me with a shuto blow, but his timing was off — just enough, partly because of the joint, partly because he slipped a little on his wet feet, and partly because of my insult to his masculinity. The sum of the partlys set his timing off just enough off for me to duck, kick him in the vitals with my right foot, and break his nose with the heel of my left hand. A little harder would have driven the bone of his nose into his brain and killed him, but there was no need for violence. He dropped to the deck.

He knew he was beat, because he knew I

could have killed him if I had wanted to. He was sucking for air and spewing blood from nose and mouth.

I let him lie there for a long count and think about plastic surgery.

I walked over to Franny, reached down and pulled her out of the Jacuzzi by her hair. I slapped the joint out of one hand and the drink out of the other.

"Jesus Christ, Alex," she looked down at Jason. "You killed him!"

"Not quite." I kicked him in the ass and he stirred. "Get your wardrobe and get out of here. Use the rear exit. You hear me, Mr. Jason?" I addressed him as mister because I wanted to leave him some dignity.

"Inside!" I shoved Franny toward the door.

Since she was already naked, it saved me the task of stripping her. I shoved her some more, straight into the shower in her bedroom. I knew right where it was. It was a big shower. We both stepped in and I turned on the cold water full blast.

I tried not to get too wet, but that didn't work out too well. I let her soak for about five minutes. I got pretty damn soaked myself.

Then I turned off the shower, grabbed a towel and pushed her into the bedroom.

She stood there dripping. Naked as April Morn. All right, September Morn. But she still looked like what she used to be, the Sex Goddess of the olden, golden days. There was something lustrous about her body that made it seem like she was moving even when she stood still. She still had it, and she knew it.

I tossed the towel at her. She held it with one hand but let it touch the floor.

"Dry off," I said.

"Do I look like that TV actress's mother to you?"

"Fairest of the Rare, Rarest of the Fair, you look great. And you can be a great actress."

"Mike sent you, didn't he?"

"Nobody sends me anywhere. I came because I wanted to come. I read that script," I lied. "He stuck his neck in a buzz saw for you when nobody else wanted you for the part. He's given you the chance to act, instead of shaking your tits and your ass and licking your tongue like . . ."

"Like what?"

"You know what. Mike Meadows might be the last decent human being in this indecent town. He sure as hell is the last one who believes you can play this part. And you piss on him. And why? Because he believes in

272

you more than you do. That's why. Because you're afraid to act. So you take the easy way and act like a slut. Goddamnit, Franny, the walls haven't come tumbling down — and neither have you, go up to Carmel and act! Really act! Show those sonofabitches what you can do with this part. Because they're the sonofabitches, not Mike Meadows."

"It's too late. I walked off."

"You can walk right back on again. No, not walk, fly. He's got a jet waiting for you. That's how much he believes in you. If you're not on that plane they're signing Ann Gavery for the part."

"Ann Gavery! Why that fat old bitch, she couldn't act . . ."

"They wanted her in the first place, everybody wanted her except Mike." I didn't know if any of that was true, but I knew she hated Gavery's guts. "That's who they want and that's who they're going to get unless you're on that plane. Get on it! Fly, Franny. Fly! Soar right into that part and reap a second glory. This is your last chance, Franny. Your last and only chance. Don't screw it up!"

She took a couple of steps closer to me and let the towel drag on the carpet. She wasn't wearing any makeup. She wasn't wearing anything. God she was still beautiful.

"You're all wet," she smiled that smile that had driven a million men crazy. Ten million.

"I'll go up," she said. She loosened my tie and started to unbutton my shirt. "But first we've got to get you dry."

What happened next is nobody's business. But she made that plane and she made that picture. And she . . . well, that's nobody's business.

Chapter Twenty-Nine

I had called Mike Meadows from Franny's place in Malibu, and he was waiting at the studio jet to take her up to Carmel himself. When she saw him and kissed him it was right out of a "B" movie, which they don't make any more except for television.

I had a feeling Frances Vale was going to give Jackie Mathews and a whole lot of other people in this jaded town a lesson in acting that they could paste in their hats. She was still the Fairest of the Rare, the Rarest of the Fair, except for my Briny Marlin.

It was too late to go back to the office and finish my novel that night, so I went home, cleaned up and changed rags. I called Myron. He was going over to see Rhoda again.

But somewhere around the time I was fetching Franny or calling Myron, there was another call taking place — between Colin Alderdyce and the man called Fedona.

"Has he called you yet?"

"Not yet, Colin. But you heard what he said. He wants it by the end of the week."

"What if he doesn't get it? What's he going to do? Go to the police?"

"No I don't think he'd do that. But that's not what we've got to worry about."

"What then?"

"What if the cops pick HIM up? What then? If they nail him for what happened to Burke, THEN we've got worries. Our best chance is if he gets out of the country."

"I never thought of that."

"Yeah, well I've been thinking. Maybe it's our best chance and maybe not. Maybe it's not our only chance."

"What do you mean?"

"I've got to think the whole thing out. I'll see you at the club on Saturday."

"Right."

"Have you talked to your mother?"

"Uh, well . . . sort of . . ."

"What the hell do you mean 'sort of'? Either you did or you didn't."

"She's not feeling so hot. Went to the doctor again, but I'll talk to her. Mike, if she doesn't come across, is there any way that you . . ."

"Don't say it, Colin. Don't even think it. I'm a businessman. And I'm not in the business of being blackmailed by some small time shithead. Just talk to your mother and I'll see you Saturday."

I drove over to Van Ness which was just a few minutes away, parked the LeBaron on the street, rang the door bell and kissed my mother hello when she opened the door.

The upstairs of the duplex was dark. It often was. She rented it to an assistant director, a nice young fellow who spent a lot of time on location out of town.

We sat at the dining room table and ate. She had prepared a varied menu of Greek victuals including a Avgolemonou soup, salad, Kiftethis, Scorthalia and Pastichia. Ever since I got there I had the feeling that there was something on her mind, something troubling her — and not the usual "when are you going to get married and settle down" stuff. After all those years, I could just tell. She was my one and only mother, and I was her one and only favorite son.

It was during the coffee and Koluria that she began to open up.

"Alex, I think I'm getting old."

"Mom, what're you talking about? Hell, you've got less gray hair than I've got."

"I'll tell you a little something about that too, Alex. Now promise me you won't say anything to anybody . . . promise?"

"Promise."

"For the last few years, I been doing a little dipping into a bottle . . . and I don't mean booze."

"You mean . . . ?" I feigned surprise.

"I mean Lady Grecian Formula."

"No!"

"Tell me the truth, Alex. You couldn't tell?"

"Hell, no!" I lied, and that made her feel better, but not for long.

"Alex, I'm thinking of selling this place and moving into an apartment or a condo. You know, one of those gated places . . ."

"But, Mom, what about the yard, the garden and the roses? You're out there most of the time. What would you do all day long . . . just vegetate?"

"I got my soaps, and . . ."

"And what?"

"Well, I think it's just too much for me . . ."

"I don't believe that. That's not true."

And it wasn't. Suddenly she looked up and shuddered. I couldn't remember the last time I saw her react like that. She heard it before I did. Maybe that's because she was expecting to hear it.

First it was a rumble, then it got louder.

"What the hell is that?"

By the time I asked, there were more noises, racing, subsiding and then reverberating and reviving again. And I could hear voices from outside. I stood up. She didn't.

"They've been coming around almost every night," she said.

"For how long?"

"About a week. Three of them. On their motorcycles. Drunk. They'll go away after a while."

By now the motors were blasting and when they did ease up, the voices came again.

"Why didn't you call the police?"

"I did. By the time they finally get here," she motioned outside, "they're gone."

"Why didn't you tell me?"

She shrugged.

"Mom, why didn't you tell me!?"

"I don't know. I just thought, maybe they'd quit coming. Go someplace else . . ."

I started for the front door.

"Alex! Leave 'em alone. They'll go away. Don't go out there!"

I went. I opened the door and stood there. There were three of them all right, in a lot of leather, shirts that no self-respecting laundry would accept, and all three wearing what looked like WW II German Army helmets. One of them was cracking about two feet of chain against the driveway.

They were surprised to see me, but I can't say that they were displeased. The odds were dominantly in their favor, particularly since I didn't have the .38 equalizer on me. They were big, dirty and drunk. But that was okay, because I was mad.

"Beat it," I said, "and don't come back."

First they laughed. No, not laughed. Cackled. A couple of them had cans of beer. "What're you doin,' layin' the old broad?" said the one with the chain.

Then they all said some things that got me madder. Things that nobody wants to hear about his mother.

"Step off that bike, asshole."

All three assholes stepped off their bikes. The one with the chain was the biggest and dirtiest. I walked down the steps and kept on coming. I learned a few things early in my dad's saloon. One thing was that whoever hits first usually wins, if he hits hard enough. They were going to taunt and talk some more. I wasn't.

Instinctively, the other guy usually looks for your right hand to make the first move. While he was looking I hit the big sonofabitch with a left, broke his nose and knocked a few teeth into his throat. He went back over his bike and both hit the pavement.

That startled both the other two. Just enough for me to kick the second one in his leather crotch, grab the third one by his leather jacket and send the hard edge of my free hand into his Adam's apple.

The second one, the one with the sore crotch, started to recover, when out of the night my mother hit him on the side of his helmet with all her might with my old Louisville Slugger baseball bat she had saved for sentimental reasons from my Little League career.

All three lay motionless amid the spilled beer.

"Call the cops now, Mom." I stooped and picked up the chain, just in case. "These guys aren't going anywhere."

She was shaking. But she smiled and nodded and walked toward the door. Lights went on next door and across the street. I guess the neighbors felt it was safe to come out.

"Mom," I called, when she got to the doorway. "Who says you're getting old?"

Chapter Thirty

The next morning I called my mother to see how she was feeling. Back in form. Not another word about moving or about last night. The only thing she was a little worried about was that I might spill the beans about her and the Grecian Formula. I set her mind at ease.

I went to the "Y" and had my usual workout and listened to the usual banter.

But my mind was not at ease. Maybe it had something to do with what happened last night. Maybe it was residual magnetism from the private eye business. Maybe it was because I still suffered from imagination constipation and couldn't face that blank sheet of paper. Whatever it was, there I was, knocking on an apartment door in Santa Monica.

The door opened. It was Tawny Tucker who opened it. Midmorning and she wore a short, short, terry cloth robe and those over-size sunglasses.

"Alex . . ."

That's as far as she got before I reached

out and took off the shades. Her left eye was still somewhat swollen and discolored. But now the right eye was shut, black and blue and puffed. So was some of the right side of her face. From that eye she had to be blind as a bean.

"He's still here, huh?"

She just lowered her head. I walked past her into the room toward Bennie Fix. He rose from the breakfast table where he was eating and watching Regis and the new girl. Bennie wore blue shorts and matching tank top. All the right bulges in all the right places.

"Yeah, I'm still here and she loves it, don't you, Tawny?"

"I told him to leave, Alex, for good . . . I swear . . ."

"Did she?" I didn't look back at her.

"Maybe she did, but she doesn't mean it, do you Tawny?" It was more of a threat than a question. "Anyhow, it's none of your goddamn business. I'm the one layin' her not you. Is that why you came around? To get laid?" He rippled his pecs a little and smirked a lot.

"No that's not why I came around." I started to look back but instead came forward with a right cross. Bennie dropped, covering his left eye.

I reached down, lifted Bennie and slugged him with a left hook. Bennie dropped again.

Dazed as he was, he managed to look upward with both hands close to his eyes.

"Night . . . are you cr . . . crazy?"

"No, Bennie. Just tit for tat." I lifted him up again. He was trembling. "Now I'll tell you what you're going to do. You're going to walk out that door. Now, while you still can."

"I . . . I . . . live here . . ."

"Not anymore."

"My clothes . . . my stuff . . ."

"It'll be out front this afternoon. You don't see her. You don't touch her. You don't call her. Because if you do I'll finish the job with gusto. Out!"

I shoved him toward the still open door. He staggered past her.

"She'll call me. You'll see!" That was Bennie Fix's exit line.

I picked up the remote and clicked off Regis and the new girl.

"Tawny, if you do, if you ever call that sonofabitch, don't ever call me."

"I won't, Alex . . . I promise. I'll never see him again . . . I can't take anymore. I just . . . can't."

She was sobbing. I went over and gently put my arms around her. She looked up with those wet, beat up eyes.

"I . . . I want to give you that five hundred . . ."

"I don't want your five hundred. Give part of it to the movers . . . and get a new life."

"I will, Alex, I promise."

I spent the rest of the morning at the office doing research by finishing *Trouble Is My Business*. Briny Marlin's door was closed. I let it stay that way and went to lunch at Johnny Rocket's.

After the hamburger and Coke I walked over to the new location of Carroll and Co. on Canon to see my friend Steve Becos who has worked for Dick and John for a few years. Maybe I'd pick up something elegant for Mrs. A.'s party. I idled among the two-thousand-dollar Chester Barrie suits, even tried on a couple.

I decided to buy a necktie instead. Some of Briny Marlin's spaghetti sauce had dripped onto my paisley. Steve sold me a sincere rep for only seventy-five dollars.

Boxed and sacked necktie in one hand, my last Lucky in the other, I stopped into Mrs. Kramer's. I didn't need pipe tobacco, but picked up a half pound of my special blend, then casually asked her to include a couple packs of Luckies to go. She glared at me, but there were several other customers in the store so this was no time for her to lecture me on the hazards of cigarette smoking. I reasonably contained a triumphant smile, nodded amiably, and went out the door and barely avoided tripping over E. Elliott Elliot's walking stick. As usual he was the most smartly attired man on the boulevard. He wore a gray-vested single-breasted suit, a blue candy-striped shirt and blue silk tie with diamond stick pin. The diamond was about the size of a fish eye but sparkled a hell of a lot more.

"Hello there, young fellow," he greeted me. "I see you have replenished your nicotine supply."

"Right."

"I gave up smoking and sex several years ago. The former on doctor's orders, the latter because I had no choice. Actually, it gave me up."

"I see."

"No, you don't. But you will someday, dear fellow. In the meantime . . ."

"Right again."

"You will find that I am invariably right. I see you've been to Carroll's. Not a bad shop but there are better. Too big for cuff links, too small to be a shirt. Either kerchiefs or necktie. Necktie."

"Yes."

"I thought as much. Do you have another date with a cop?"

"No, Elliott. This time it's with Aphrodite."

"Congratulations. Have you lunched?"

"Yes."

"Where?"

"Johnny Rocket's."

"God in heaven!"

"Why? Are you just going to lunch."

"Hardly. I've just spent two hours at The Polo, one of my five favorite restaurants in Beverly Hills. Magnificent food with mediocre company. My agent who is trying to sell me down the river again. Something called television. Have you ever heard of it?"

"Vaguely."

A beige Bentley was double-parked nearby with the motor running and a chauffeur at the wheel.

"Isn't that your Bentley?" I pointed.

"It is, and my man Carstairs."

"What's he doing? Following you?"

"Yes."

"Why?"

"He always does when I take my afternoon constitutional among the colonials."

"Why?"

"In case I tire of pedestrian society — you

may take that any way you choose — Carstairs is always at the ready."

"Handy."

"Isn't it." He pointed with his walking stick toward the WRITERS AND ARTISTS BUILDING. "Are you on your way back to the *oubliette?*"

"I am."

"I see. Well, I'm heading in the opposite direction at the moment, just to see what's afoot."

"So long, Elliott."

"Give Aphrodite my . . . regards."

"I'll do that."

This time I knocked on Aphrodite's door.

"Come in, come in, whoever you are."

"I are Alex Night," I said opening the door, "and I are just checking on our date."

"Why? Do you want to back out?"

"Back out?! My dear woman, I can not tell you with what anticipation I look forward to spending this night with you."

"This evening," she reproved.

"A little slip."

"There's no such thing as a little slip, a little pregnant, or a little garlic."

"I stand corrected," I bowed. "And admonished."

"Duly noted." She nodded toward the

Carroll sack. "What have you got there?"

"My, my. You sound just like Elliott, but don't look anything like him, I'm happy to say. Is it bad luck for a beau to show his date the necktie he's going to wear before the ceremony?"

"I don't think so."

"I'm not going to take a chance. Is seven-forty-five agreeable?"

"Agreeable."

"In the meantime, if you need anything, just whistle. I'll be right across the hall. And if you don't like this necktie, do you know what I'm going to do with it?"

"What?"

"Hang myself."

"I'll like it. I'll like it."

Chapter Thirty-One

I went through the scrubbing, shaving and Brut-splashing routine all over again. I picked out the most expensive of my five suits and topped it off with my new seventy-five-dollar foulard.

Late that afternoon I had the LeBaron washed again and at seven-forty I parked it on the street and walked up to squire my Aphrodite.

She looked even better that night than she had on Wednesday. Just a touch of evening make-up and she smelled fresh as a dawn meadow.

"Good evening, Briny Marlin."

"Good evening, New Neck Tie."

At seven-forty-eight we approached the LeBaron parked on the street — under a tree.

If I could say the word and destroy every bird in the world, I would say that word.

Smack in the middle of my windshield was a splattered white pattern right out of a Rorschach.

"Birds do it," she smiled.

"They sure as hell do." I didn't smile.

As we headed toward Beverly Hills I turned on the radio. Frank Sinatra was singing "Come Fly With Me."

"You like Sinatra?" I asked.

"Sure."

"They say more babies were conceived when couples listened to his songs than to any other music."

"I thought it was Ravel's *Bolero*, and can we change the subject?"

"Sure. Where you from?"

"Stamford, Connecticut."

"Lot of Greeks in Stamford?"

"Quite a few, but my mother was Irish, Colleen Ryan."

"That's some combination. Greek and Irish. They live in Stamford now?"

"Died there. Automobile accident. They were sober, the other driver was drunk. He lived, they didn't."

"Sorry."

"Hey, you didn't tell me much about the party. Who's our host?"

"Hostess. Cynthia Alderdyce."

"Oh! Isn't she the lady in the newspaper story? The lady whose jewels you defended?"

"That's one way of putting it, though I

think she could have defended them all by herself."

"You sound like you like her."

"I do. She's a real spicy tomato. Used to be a chorus girl at the old Copacabana in New York. Don't know what she was before that. Married an oil man, a wildcatter. Just like Clark Gable in *Boom Town*. They lived happily ever after, until he died. I don't think she's so happy any more. But she doesn't let it show."

As we turned left on Ambassador Drive I saw that there was a valet parking service set up in front of the Alderdyce residence.

I gave the guy a five-dollar bill and asked him to do something about the windshield. He promised he would. Later I found out that he did. He smeared it.

Inside, the place glittered. The "little party" was just about in full sway. Forty people there and some still coming. People mixing and munching from the sumptuous buffet. Music came from somewhere. Nice romantic music, just like the mood I was in. Most of the men mixers were conservatively dressed, but there were a few in designer jeans and St. Lauren loose casualtees.

The older women also were dressed conservatively and expensively. The younger ladies were mostly overexposed and over made up. Low décolletage, high skirts. Except Goldie.

Several celebrities mingled among the anonymous. Zsa Zsa again, R. J. Wagner with Jill, Ernie and Toda, Charles and Kim Bronson, Anne Francis, Angie Dickinson, Jamie Farr, and a few studio and network executives that I recognized. There were a couple of rock singers that I didn't. Some of the people seemed to be more interested in the architecture than the festivities.

Peter and several others in help were attending to the beverage requirements of the guests from two bars set up strategically. My old pal Peter approached us. Goldie and I both had plates in our hands.

"May I get you a drink, Mr. Night?"

"Not right now Peter, thanks."

"And the lady?" he inquired.

"No thank you," said the lady. Peter nodded and moved off.

Later, Goldie made an exception about martinis away from home and she and I each had one, not nearly as good as I mix, and we were concentrating on the food.

"Good eats," she pointed to her plate.

"Good company," I pointed to her. "But know what? I liked our Wednesday night party a lot better."

"The evening is young." She smiled.

That too, was promising.

As we both turned, I bumped into Ernie Borgnine. Borgnine is friendly to a fault. He has only one other fault. He can't remember anybody's name. He had co-starred with Mitchum in *The Old Dick*, the detective movie on which, nominally, I was the technical advisor.

Mr. B. can read a page of dialogue just a couple of times and shoot the scene without kicking a line, but when it comes to names he shoots blanks.

"Hi . . . pal," he grinned.

"Hello, Alex," his beautiful wife Tova smiled. We had only met once when she visited the set years ago.

"How have you been, Alex?" Ernie picked up the cue.

Funny thing about Borgnine, in the old days when he played Marty and won the Academy Award, when he was Fatso in *From Here to Eternity* and in all those other fifties and sixties pictures, he could have been charitably described as homely. Since he met and married Tova over twenty years ago, he's somehow segued from homely to handsome.

I introduced Goldie to the Borgnines and we chatted pleasantly until they were surrounded by other people whose names Tova pronounced loudly and clearly.

"Hey," Goldie motioned. "Isn't that Jamie Farr?"

"That's his nose."

"I loved him in *M*A*S*H*. You know him?"

"He's a nice guy," I nodded.

"Do you know a lot of these people?"

"Some of them used to be my clients, when I was in the detective business."

"I'll bet you know a lot of dirt."

"It was a dirty business. Well, look who's here."

E. Elliott Elliot had made a late entrance, evidently checked his walking stick at the door and approached us directly and grandly. He wore an impeccably tailored suit and a look of disdain.

"Good evening, fellow scribblers," he greeted.

"Elliott," I said, "you didn't mention that you were invited tonight."

"Dear boy," he intoned. "In Beverly Hills no one would dream of not inviting me."

"No one over seventy," Jamie Farr, who was passing by and overheard, remarked.

"Jamie," Elliott replied, "are you 'butling' here tonight? I'm delighted to see that you've found employment."

"Good evening, Alex," Jamie smiled at me. "Goodnight, Elliott," and he headed for the buffet. Peter appeared at Elliott's elbow.

"Mr. Elliot," Peter bowed slightly, "may I get you a drink?"

"I'll have the usual, Peter."

"Very good, sir." Peter went off to implement the order, whatever it was.

Elliott looked about imperiously, surveying the scene. A few passersby greeted him, mostly the geriatric set, by name. He barely acknowledged their salutation, by nod, not by word, and continued his scrutiny.

"That's interesting," he said as his eyes settled on a foursome at a corner.

"What is?" Goldie asked, not to disappoint him.

"You see that fat fellow to our distant right? The one with the wrinkled lapels?"

Goldie and I both nodded and nibbled.

"Martin Fenimore. The woman next to him, the retread with the blue hair and blonde eyes, is his wife. She's been under the knife more frequently than that Diller woman."

"What's so interesting about that?" Goldie kept feeding him cues.

"The young tart his wife is talking to, the

one accompanied by the thin fellow most likely wearing women's underwear, is Fenimore's mistress."

"My, my," I exclaimed. "Do such things happen in Beverly Hills?"

"He happens to have her stashed in an apartment on Charleville just off Beverly Drive."

"Is that so?" I said. "How often does he visit her?"

"Dear fellow, don't be so damn nosy."

Peter returned with Elliott's usual. Elliott sipped and looked about again.

"Terrible, isn't it." He clucked.

"What, the drink?" I knew that wasn't what he meant.

"No. This 'affair.' "

"Come on, Elliott, I think it's a very elegant party." Goldie smiled.

" 'Party,' indeed. More like a real estate open house — for a select few, of course. A garage sale, only the house goes with the garage."

"What the hell are you talking about, Elliott?" Whatever it was, I didn't appreciate the implication.

"Dear boy, those of us 'in the know,' know that Cynthia Alderdyce, poor old girl, is in dire financial straits."

"Elliott, sometimes your wit gets in the

way of facts. Cynthia Alderdyce just happens to be . . ."

"In dire financial straits, I repeat. I count at least half a dozen prospective buyers among the guests. The rest of us are just window dressing — atmosphere, shills — like that fellow in women's underwear."

"You're nuts."

"Am I?" He pointed to the backyard with the huge pool and tennis court. "Why do you think the great outdoors is burning with light?"

The pool, tennis court and the entire area were all illuminated.

"The better for would-be buyers to see by on a relatively chilly night. That handsome blonde lady talking so earnestly to that brummagem businessman from Minneapolis is Lucy Ann Bell, top salesperson at Coldwell Banker Real Estate. Of course I'm not certain he's from Minneapolis. That Korean couple swooping about certainly isn't."

"I don't believe it," I said even though maybe I was beginning to. The truth is, I just didn't want to believe it.

"Oh, you can believe it all right. You've heard it from an unimpeachable source."

Damn you, Elliott, I thought to myself. Damn you and your smart, smug, snide sophistry — your know-it-all nose in Cynthia Alderdyce's business. I almost said something about it, but didn't. And now I'm glad I didn't. It wasn't Elliott's fault. He was just the messenger, if it was true. But true or not, I hoped Elliott wouldn't spread it around. Most people here didn't know, and I didn't want them to know.

"Where is Cynthia?" Elliott sipped and babbled on. "I haven't seen her yet."

I looked outside and saw the white swan floating in the shimmering pool. The swan seemed proud and at peace in its untroubled little world. That swan always reminded me of Cynthia Alderdyce. But maybe Cynthia wasn't at peace. Maybe her world was falling apart.

"Goldie," I said. "You want to go outside and get a little fresh air?"

She nodded and we left Elliott standing and sipping his drink amidst the Beverly Hills cognoscenti.

At that moment Cynthia Alderdyce was not at peace. She was in the library with Colin. I'm not exactly sure about the conversation, but from what I pieced together later on, I can guess the content.

"Colin, for the last time it is impossible. There has to be some other way."

"There isn't any other way. The only way is for me to deliver fifty thousand dollars by this weekend. If I don't . . ."

"Well you won't. I can't raise that kind of money by this weekend. I can't raise it at all. Can't you understand we are extended. No, not extended. We are broke."

"Borrow on the insurance."

"I already have. The only way to get more is if I die."

"Mother . . ."

"I've been mother and father and nursemaid to you since your father died. But now it's over. I've sold the desert house, but it was mortgaged to the hilt. I'm trying to sell this place. The banks just aren't lending. There are a hundred places for sale in Beverly Hills, more than a hundred. Even if I can sell it, it takes time."

"He won't wait!"

"He'll have to."

"Sell the jewels."

"I already have."

"They're gone?"

"They will be. They're still in the safe but they don't belong to us, to me, anymore. Nothing does except this house. That's all that's left."

"I don't believe it!"

"All right, I'm lying to you."

"I didn't mean it that way, Mother."

"Just like you didn't mean all those marriages, all those stupid business schemes, all the times I've supported you and tried to keep up pretenses and hoped for a miracle. Well, there are no miracles, Colin. There just aren't any. So for once you'll have to make other arrangements. Now, we've been away from our guests too long. One of them might even want to buy the joint."

Goldie and I were outside. I guess I was staring at the floating swan.

"It is beautiful," she said.

"What?"

"I said this place, it's beautiful."

"Yeah."

"Have you been here often?"

"Pretty often, mostly on business. I was here just a couple of days ago."

"On business?"

"No. Because a nice old lady wanted to do something nice. Hey, you've got goose bumps, beautiful goose bumps, but we'd better get inside and have a nice cold martini. That ought to warm you up." I started to lead her toward the party.

"Alex," she paused by the pool.

"What?"

"You're aces."

She kissed me on the lips but barely and just for a moment.

"Just call me Mr. Lucky."

We walked back into the house.

Elliott was talking to Mrs. A. and Colin. Mrs. A. waved to me so we went over. As we approached, Elliott was starting to move away.

"Oh there's Sylvia Ashley," he was saying. "She's a terrible bore but there's something I've got to find out from her." He went to find out something.

"Good evening, Mrs. Alderdyce," I said. "This is Goldie Rose. Thanks for inviting us. Oh, Goldie, Colin Alderdyce."

"A pleasure, Miss Rose." I thought the bastard was going to kiss her hand or anything else he could get hold of. It must have showed because Miss Sweden appeared from the wings in a flash and her blue eyes were definitely green.

"Colin," the Valkyrie gritted and grabbed his arm. "I've been looking for you. Let's get a drink." She led him away without a hello or a good-bye to Goldie or me. Especially Goldie.

"Miss Rose," Mrs. A. smiled. "I'm so glad that you were able to be here, and that is a very nice gentleman you're with."

"Thank you. I know it."

"You two enjoy yourselves," said Mrs. A. and there was a sort of misty look in her eyes when she said it. "Enjoy yourselves every minute." That was as close to losing her equanimity as I had ever seen her, even on that night when a gun was pointing at her.

"Mrs. Alderdyce," I couldn't help asking. "Is everything all right?"

"What a question." She composed herself immediately. "Of course it is."

"Mrs. A.," I wanted to change the complexion of things, "I have that . . . that paper you asked about."

"Oh yes, well Alex, things are a bit hectic here tonight. Would you mind coming by at say two, tomorrow afternoon? There's something else I want to talk to you about."

"Sure, two'll be fine."

"Good. Now there are some people that I have to see. Miss Rose, please come visit us again."

"Thank you."

I couldn't help notice that Cynthia Alderdyce walked toward Lucy Ann Bell and the Korean couple.

On the way back from Ambassador Drive, KGRB was playing Sinatra again. Only now Sinatra was younger and singing "There Are Such Things."

I wasn't very good company. A couple of times Goldie made some comment about the party, but my response didn't do much to keep the conversation running. She is a very perceptive young woman, so we listened to Sinatra.

I parked the LeBaron under the same tree and didn't much care if the birds did it again. She took my hand as we walked up to her door, but let go of it to get her key. She opened the door, put the key back in her purse and we both took a step inside.

Without putting her arms around me she kissed me that poolside kiss — only a little more. When we came apart she smiled.

"Your lips may be here, but . . ."

"Huh?"

"The lyrics to that song, '. . . where is your heart?' " She smiled. "With a nice old lady up there on Ambassador Drive?"

"I am sorry." I said it and I meant it. This just wasn't fair, not to Briny Marlin.

"And maybe I am a little jealous. You really like her, don't you?"

"That I do."

"So do I."

"Good. But watch out for sonny boy."

"Colin?"

"That's the only sonny boy she's got."

"I think he's got his hands full with that

Swedish smorgasbord — and she does look like a handful, or didn't you notice?"

"I only have eyes for you." I moved closer and put my arms around her. "Do you mind if I try again?"

"If at first you don't succeed . . ."

I gave her the mid-Night special.

"Succ . . . ess," she said.

"Ditto."

We did it again. And while we were doing it, her leg moved from her knee down and with the heel of her shoe she nudged the door closed.

"Would you like . . ." our lips were still touching ". . . to come in?"

This time I did see her bedroom. Only it wasn't a bedroom. It was a magic carpet. A magic bullet. It was all the love songs ever sung. All the poems ever written. All the movies ever made.

A trip to the moon on gossamer wings: Earth Had Not Anything To Show More Fair. Boom Town. Fools Rush In. How Do I Love Thee? The Man Who Came To Dinner. Dancing In The Dark. Hail To Thee Blithe Spirit. Heaven's Gate. The Great Love Story That's Never Been Told. Harlot's House. Everything You've Ever Wanted To Know About Sex. Do It Again. Little Lamb, Who Made Thee? Jaws. Something To Remember You By. Ode To A Grecian Urn. Night Of The Hunter. There's No Tomorrow. Sweet And Low. Grand Illusion.

Words and music. Rhythm and rhyme. The sins of cinema.

Earlier that night Cynthia Alderdyce had said, "Enjoy yourselves. Every minute."

We did just that . . . and then some.

Chapter Thirty-Two

There must have been something about the way I walked, or whistled or something the next morning. Three or four guys at the "Y" kept asking my why the hell I was so happy. When I looked into the mirror to shave there did appear to be a sort of goofy look on the face grinning back at me. Like somebody who had made four the hard way — two deuces.

I took a good long steam that morning but there was something in my system that I didn't want to get out. Goldie and I hadn't talked much that night. But we'd have to some time. Probably soon.

Maybe neither of us planned it. Maybe both of us did. But I had a feeling that it wouldn't happen again before we talked things out. I wasn't ready to go buy a wedding ring and she might've tossed it back at me if I did. But we did have to come to some sort of understanding. Before I left she told me she might not come in in the morning, but she'd see me sometime during the day.

When I got to the office Morgan Nobel was just returning Elliott's trade papers which she had borrowed again without his knowledge. As she placed them on the floor in front of his door the Bernstein brothers walked out of the men's room. They even went to the toilet together.

"Morning Morgan," said Bruce. "What's new . . . ?"

". . . in the trades," said Bernie, "this fine day?"

"I never read that left-wing trash," Morgan replied and marched toward her end of the hall.

"Don't forget the Klan meeting tonight," said Bruce.

"Ten o'clock sharp," said Bernie. "Bring matches."

I went into my office and took off my jacket. The building felt almost like home. There was something warm about the cold, old, creaking structure, an architectural anomaly among the new, more elegant buildings. The stories that must have been written there. Poems, plays, novels, movies and television pilots and episodes. Comedy and drama. Heartbreak and triumph. This old building had spawned thousands of stories from hundreds of writers.

Some of the writers were ghosts now. But

that's the great thing about putting something on paper. Even when you're gone it's still there. What you liked and didn't like. The characters that you create never die. They live and speak and love and hate forever. The written word is eternal.

This building and the people in it, with its great cross-section of the writing world, had contributed memorably to the fine art of writing — everybody but me.

My contribution consisted of a single sheet of paper with a title, plus one sentence.

I started to write.

The phone rang. It was Myron Garter who wanted to know if I wanted to have lunch. I told him I'd meet him at the Mandarin Wok at noon.

The Mandarin Wok has a rather modest entrance on Beverly Drive between Brighton Way and Little Santa Monica. But when you walk inside and go downstairs it's not so modest. There is a comfortable bar in a section to the left and there are different levels of booths and tables for lunch and dinner.

For nine and a half dollars they have an excellent oriental buffet including salad, chicken, sweet and sour pork, several beef dishes, shrimp, egg rolls, mushrooms, pods and a dazzling array of desserts — all you can eat. That's why Myron Garter liked to eat there.

But not that day. He still liked it, but he didn't eat much. He had something else on his mind and it wasn't the crime rate in Beverly Hills.

"I took Rhoda home today. Not my home, ours. Well it used to be ours, it's hers now. She's changed a lot since that night . . . that night when we met and had dinner. She was hysterical that night. She seems a lot more composed now. I guess when you almost die, it does things to you. You know what I mean, Alex?"

Maybe I did, and maybe I didn't.

"She says she's going to quit the damn pills. All of them, cold turkey. I believe her. She's got a strong will when she puts her mind to it. She says she's going to lose weight too. Go to a fat farm maybe. I told her, 'Go, Rhoda, go ahead and go. Get away from here for a while.' You know she's got that income from the money her mother and father left her. So that's no problem. You know, Alex, she never took a penny of alimony from me, not a penny. 'Course she kept the house, but her mother and dad put down the down payment, anyhow. I wanted to pay them back but they wouldn't hear of it. Said it was her money anyhow. They didn't have any other kids.

"But she says she's probably going to sell the house, leave all that behind. Start all over. I think that's probably a good idea, don't you, Alex?"

I agreed that that probably was a good idea, and I listened to him talk and not overstuff himself for the first time since — well, since a couple of years ago.

He probably would have kept on talking but I told him that I had a two o'clock date with Mrs. Alderdyce and if I didn't get a move on I'd be late.

Myron Garter said he'd call me later.

At exactly one-fifty-eight I rang the chimes on Ambassador Drive. It took Peter less than four seconds to respond by opening the door. He bade me enter. I did.

The place had been cleaned up and there was no visible evidence of the sales campaign, if that's what it had been.

Peter told me that Mrs. Alderdyce was expecting me. I already knew that. He also told me that she was outside in the patio area. I would have guessed that she'd be in the library. The afternoon was a little unfriendly for California. There was a chill on the hill. I followed the family retainer outdoors and greeted the lady of the house. Cynthia Alderdyce looked tired and thinner. But she smiled that gracious smile.

"Good afternoon, Alex. Would you like coffee?"

"No, thank you. That was a swell party, Mrs. A."

"Wasn't it. And Alex, I hope you're serious about that young lady, Miss Rose. She's got something. I can tell. I'm a wise old party, Alex."

"I know you are."

"In some things," she added. "But not so wise in others."

I let that pass.

"Sure you won't have coffee?"

"I'm sure."

"Then let's take a little stroll again." She rose and looked around the yard and up toward the hills. "My husband loved to walk. 'Come on, Cyn,' he'd say. 'Let's go for a good stretch of the legs.' Did I ever tell you that you remind me of him? Of course I did. He was a big man, a man who could leap upon mountains. On an oil derrick or at the Astor, he was a man people noticed. The first time he went broke after we were married, he took me to a park and bought a bag of peanuts with the last dime in his pocket. He poured some of those peanuts in my hand and said, 'Cyn, next year, they'll be diamonds. I promise.'

"He kept that promise. He kept every promise he ever made. Oh, forgive me, Alex, I didn't ask you here to listen to the babbling of a silly old woman." She took hold of my left hand in both of hers. They were cold. "It's just that I don't have anyone to talk to . . ."

She didn't finish. She knew what I was thinking. But I didn't say it.

"Your hands are cold," I said instead. "You sure you don't want to go inside?"

"No. Let's keep walking."

"Okay." I fished the sheet on Burke from my inside pocket. "Here's the information on James Wesley Burke and I'm pretty sure I know who the accomplice was and who probably . . ."

"Alex," she interrupted and stopped walking. Cynthia Alderdyce spoke with a different voice. "I want you to listen and listen carefully. These are my instructions. I want you to forget about the robbery, about Burke, or whatever his name is, and about his accomplice."

"Mrs. A. . . ."

"I want you to forget about everything and anybody having to do with this situation."

"I don't understand, just a couple days ago . . ."

"Things have changed!" She flared. "I don't want you or anyone else prying into my affairs. Can you understand that, you damned idiot!"

She may as well have hit me with a ballpeen hammer. Getting shot didn't hurt me as much, and she realized it as soon as she said it.

"All right. Anything you say. No more prying . . ."

"Oh, Alex, my dear . . ." She put her arms around me. ". . . I'm so sorry. You know I didn't mean that."

I knew it. I also knew that as tough as she was, even her endurance was being stretched to the breaking point. I wanted to do everything I could to keep her from breaking. But there were some things I had to find out.

"Am I forgiven?" she asked.

"Mrs. A. . . . is this place for sale?"

"How did you find out? Still the detective, eh, Alex?" She smiled.

"It's just my nature. But after last night, it didn't take much of a detective . . ."

"I don't suppose it was very subtle, was it?" She looked toward the inflated rubber swan floating in the pool. "Alex, it won't matter much longer . . . not for me."

If she had stunned me before, this one just

about brought me to my knees.

"It's some damn thing I can't even pronounce. Some kind of cancer. The doctors say that it'll be quick . . ."

"I'm sorry . . ."

"Don't be. I've lived every minute." She looked right into my eyes and damn near smiled. "You know, Alex, for oh, maybe the past year, every day I've had the feeling that I was getting closer to Alan."

That was the first time that I could remember her mentioning her husband by his name.

"I can almost touch him and hear him saying, 'Come on, Cyn, let's go for a good stretch of the legs.' Promise me, Alex, that no matter what happens you won't feel sorry for me."

I didn't say a word. I couldn't, not without making a fool of myself. I just nodded.

"Now just one more thing. Promise that you'll do as I asked. Will you do that?"

I reached into my pocket, pulled out the sheet on Burke and tore it up. Then I stuffed it back into the pocket.

"Thanks," she smiled. "Tough guy."

And she kissed me.

Chapter Thirty-Three

I went back to the office and lay on the Naugahyde couch without any pretense of doing any writing.

I wasn't thinking about plots, or fictional characters and private eyes, or murders and mystery stories. I was thinking of a sweet old lady dying. And I thought of a poem we had to memorize in high school. It was called "Thanatopsis," Greek for "death." It was written by William Cullen Bryant, and for some reason it stuck with me. Maybe because I had faced death too many times. But I was still alive. Cynthia Alderdyce wasn't going to be, not for long. But she faced death the way the poet described:

> So live, that when thy summons
> comes to join
> The innumerable caravan which moves
> To that mysterious realm, where
> each shall take
> His chamber in the silent halls of
> death,

*Thou go not, like the quarry-slave
at night,
Scourged to his dungeon, but
sustained and soothed
By and unfaltering trust, approach
thy grave,
Like one that wraps the drapery of
his couch
About him, and lies down to
pleasant dreams.*

Cynthia Alderdyce had an unfaltering trust. A trust that she'd be with her wild-catter again. I hoped that that trust was true. But she shouldn't have to go like this. Not alone. She had a son. But I wondered if she had even told her son. Somehow I had the feeling that she told me first.

I thought about Colin Alderdyce and wondered where he was and what he was doing while his mother was home telling me that she was dying.

Later I found out. Colin Alderdyce was playing tennis.

The game was doubles. Colin and Ingrid versus Mike Fedona and a young brunette. The game ended when Colin served an ace and winning point past the brunette.

317

"Game!" Ingrid double bounced on her side of the court.

"I'm beat," said the brunette. "In more ways than one."

"Let's play another set," Fedona swung his racket through the air.

"You men play," the brunette started to walk off the court. "I'm going to take a shower. Meet you at the bar, Mike." She looked back. "You coming, Ingrid?"

"I guess so," Miss Sweden shrugged. "The three of us can't play." She walked off the court with the brunette. Ingrid's shorts and halter were borderline dress code for the club and some of the men on the other courts did a lot of noticing. They had been noticing all afternoon.

First Fedona, then Colin Alderdyce walked to the sidelines. They each picked up a towel and dried off. Colin looked around and made sure nobody was within earshot. After Ingrid had walked away nobody paid any attention to the two men.

"What're we going to do, Mike? There's no way that I can get that money. No way."

"You won't have to."

"What?!"

"I've been thinking."

"You said that before."

"This time I've got it all worked out. He

called this morning. Wants the money, eleven o'clock tonight."

"Tonight!"

"That's when he wants it. He's going to call again at five o'clock and confirm that I've got it, but . . ."

"But what? We HAVEN'T got it!"

"He doesn't know that. But even if we had it and paid him off this time, you know what'll happen? When it's gone he'll come back again . . . and again. He'll own us."

"What's the alternative?"

"Another kind of payoff."

"What're you talking about?"

Fedona stopped drying. He walked to the water cooler. Colin followed.

"The man's a thief. He's going to get caught in the act."

"What act?"

"Leave it to me. It happened once before when somebody tried to rob the place."

"Jesus Christ, Mike!"

"I introduced you to him in the first place, him and Burke . . ."

"But Mike, I . . ."

"No buts. He's screwing around with the wrong guy." Fedona extracted a paper cup from the cooler container. "Back where I come from we don't let people get away with this kind of shit."

"I don't know, Mike . . ."

"I do."

Fedona pushed the cooler button, filled the paper container and drank half the cup.

"Colin. There just isn't any other way." Fedona drank the other half.

"I'm not going to be there, I just can't . . ."

"Who said you had to be there? You just stay home. Damn, I'm thirsty." He filled the cup again and this time swallowed all the water at once. "Stay home, Colin. You and I will settle up later."

I don't know how long I lay on the Naugahyde couch, at least I didn't know then. My thoughts drifted from Cynthia Alderdyce to my mother who also was getting pretty old, to Myron Garter and the redeemed — maybe — Rhoda, to E. Elliott Elliot and the other "scribblers" in the three-story writing factory we all shared in Beverly Hills. What a cockeyed cocoon. But through it all I saw her face before me. Goldie Rose — Briny Marlin.

Cynthia Alderdyce had told me to forget all about the robbery and Burke and Mason, even through she didn't even know his name. Those were her instructions.

I usually have a disdain for discipline. But

this time I was going to do as I was in-structed. Cynthia Alderdyce was facing her destiny. I had to face mine. She knew hers. I sure as hell didn't know mine. I didn't know if it included Goldie Rose.

It did at the moment. When I looked up from the couch she was standing at the door.

Chapter Thirty-Four

"Come in, Briny Marlin. Come in," I said and rose from the couch. "That's what new doors are for."

She stepped in and closed the new door. She had never done that before. She looked as if she had been racing against nature all day. Her hair was wind-blown, her face a little red from the sun. She wore no lipstick or eye makeup. She looked like the fire of Spring — and beautiful.

We must have looked at each other for at least a full minute without saying anything. For one of the few times in my life I wanted to be careful. I didn't want to be clever, or funny or flip . . . but I was afraid of being maudlin. She rescued me from my mini-dilemma.

"Alex, put your arms around me. Hold me for just a minute."

I kept my mouth shut and did what I was asked to do. She felt good, very good and in those few seconds it brought back all of last night. I thought that maybe that's what she wanted, to be reassured that it happened and that I still felt the same way. I still didn't say anything.

She pulled back just a little. I let go. She walked to the window then turned and looked at me. She was framed against the window and back-lit so her face was almost in shadow.

"Alex, right after I got up this morning I went for a ride. I just got back."

"Where did you go?"

"Geographically, up along the coast, up to Santa Barbara. I even stopped at an old Spanish mission. I went inside. There was nobody there. I mean . . . there were no other people.

"For the first time in a long while, I guess since my mother and father died, I knelt and I prayed. I didn't pray to be forgiven for my sins. I don't believe in that. I think that God, if there is a God, doesn't listen to that 'I'm sorry' stuff and 'I'll never do it again.' You don't show that you're sorry by mumbling a few words and crossing yourself. If you're sorry you show it in other ways. By what you do, or don't do from then on.

"Don't get me wrong, Alex. I'm not sorry about last night. Not one bit. It was the sweetest, the best, the most wonderful thing that's happened to me since, well since I grew up and lost my childhood faith.

"It's not because of what happened, at least not what happened between us. It's because I'm afraid of what might happen if I let go and let it happen again. I made a mistake with a man once before. He was sweet and gentle and thoughtful. Until we were married.

"I was just starting to be successful and he wasn't. So I guess he had to show me and himself that he could be successful at something else. The first time it happened, I left him. He followed me and told me he was sorry, promised it would never happen again. For some reason I believed him. I wanted to believe him. The next time it was worse. He was drunk, and afterward he left me bleeding and unconscious and went to sleep.

"He kept a gun. When I came to, I got the gun out of the drawer, walked over to the bed, held it an inch from his head and squeezed the trigger.

"But I just didn't squeeze hard enough to pull the trigger. Looking back, maybe I didn't want to squeeze hard enough. At the time I thought I did. But I came that close. And so did he. That close to changing my life and ending his.

"I haven't touched a gun since. Or a man. Until last night. Alex, I never thought I could put all of that behind me, but I did. You did it for me. And I'll never forget it, and I thank you for it, no matter what happens. And no matter what happens we'll have last night. But I'm still a little afraid to let go.

"On the way back I stopped and walked out to a rocky little cove along the beach. Somehow I felt even closer to God there than I did at the mission. I thought of that poem, 'Dover Beach,' and I remembered the last few lines: 'Let us be true to one another. For the world which seems to lie before us like a land of dreams, so various, so beautiful, so new, hath really neither joy, nor love, nor light, nor certitude nor peace, nor help for pain; And we are here as on a darkling plain, swept with confused alarms of struggle and flight where ignorant armies clash by night.'

"Alex, the only thing I ask, the only thing I'm saying is, let us be true to one another, truthful. In spite of last night I don't know that much about you. What I do know, what I have seen, I like very much. Very much. But I also know there's been a lot of violence in your life. I can't take any more violence. I can't have it turned toward me. I don't know what I'd do if that ever happened again.

"Alex, can you understand that?"

I understood. And I understood the tears that she was trying to hold back and couldn't. I walked close to her and put both of my hands on her face as gently as I knew how. And then I kissed her as gently as I knew how.

"Before I'd hurt you, Briny Marlin, I'd . . . I don't know what I'd do. No matter what I say, no matter what I do, it'll be the truth."

"I think I know that. And I think we don't ever have to mention it again." She smiled and winked. "Now, shall I go out that brand new door and come back in again?"

"I've got a better idea." I took her in my arms and kissed her and we both got that old feeling. "You like my idea?"

"Can't you give a lady a chance to make up her mind?"

"How long will it take?"

"I don't know. How long have you got?"

"Well, let's see I've got until . . ."

The phone rang.

"Let's discuss it over dinner. I know a good steak house . . ."

The phone kept on ringing.

"Aren't you going to answer it?"

"Nope."

"It might be your favorite cop," she smiled.

"I'll ditch him." I started to pick up the phone.

"Or your mother."

"I'll ditch her too. Hello."

"Night? Alex Night?"

The voice was familiar.

"That's right."

"This is Frank Mason."

"Well, hello 'Sport.' What can I do for you?"

"You can meet me alone tonight."

"Say again."

"Listen good because I got no time for games. You can meet me alone tonight at nine — no cops — no wire — just the two of us."

"You must think I'm a little nuts, Mase ol' Sport. Why would I do that?"

"Because that's the only way you'll ever find out what Colin Alderdyce had to do with that heist out in the desert. Him and Fedona."

The sonofabitch had me and he knew it. That's about the only chum he could have tossed out that I would have gone for. But I didn't want to go for it too fast. I gave it a little dramatic pause.

"Night, I said I wasn't going to waste time playing games. You want to know about

Alderdyce and Fedona or not? You've got five seconds."

"Maybe I am a little nuts. Where?"

"What kind of a car do you drive?"

"LeBaron, convertible."

"Drive it up to Fox Hill Lane just off Mandeville Canyon. Know where that is?"

"Right."

"At nine o'clock park under the fourth street light from the corner."

"Fourth light. Okay."

"Get out and wait on the driver's side. Make sure it's the driver's side. Now I'm telling you. Come — and bring a thousand dollars cash."

"A thousand."

"It'll be worth it. Can you do that?"

"I can do that."

"Do it!" He hung up.

I looked at the phone, then looked at Goldie who was smiling a kittenish smile.

"That wasn't your mother," she said.

I shook my head "no."

"And it wasn't a cop."

I shook my head again and hung up the phone.

"And you didn't ditch him."

I just shrugged.

"And we're not going to that steak house tonight."

"How does tomorrow night sound?"

"You know something?" She walked up close. Very close. "I like your 'I suppose.' " She touched my nose with the tip of her finger.

"That's good."

"You know something else?"

"What?"

"I like your 'north and south.' " She touched my lips, not with her finger.

Chapter Thirty-Five

I didn't intend to die that night. But let's put it this way — if I were Prudential or Equitable I wouldn't have sold me any life insurance.

Goldie knew that I wasn't going bowling, or to a basketball game, or to sit in on a game of nickel and dime poker. But she didn't give me any of that "be careful, Alex" business.

After last night and what happened in the office that afternoon I wanted to live a long, happy, useful existence, and not alone. I wanted to buy a boat. It didn't have to be much of boat, a small boat would do just fine. And I'd paint "Briny Marlin" on the side of it and take a trip. A nice slow trip. It didn't even have to be to China. Catalina would do just fine. Oh, and I'd want to take somebody along. Maybe even the kids.

Maybe I was way off course. But that's the way that I was thinking. I kissed Goldie one last time at the office, but I did my best to make it seem like a goodnight kiss, not good-bye. I told her I might call her later at home. If it got too late I'd call her the next morning. That would be Sunday and we might have breakfast and go for a drive, this time together, along the ocean, or up to Arrowhead or — hell, I didn't care where. I just wanted to be there with her.

She went into her office and I went home. I laid out some cold cuts, Greek olives, cheese and sourdough bread, and washed it all down with a Coke. I didn't want to drink any booze.

Then I took a shower. If I did turn out to be a corpse, I could at least be clean.

After I got dressed, I got completely dressed. I took the .38 Special out of its shoulder holster and tucked it into my belt. Mase had said "no cops" — "no wire." He didn't say anything about a couple of pounds of loaded hardware. But there was something else he mentioned. One thousand dollars.

I kept twenty crisp one-hundred-dollar bills in a special safe depository for special occasions — fast getaways, fast bribes, maybe even a fast funeral. My mother was the only other person who knew about the special safe depository.

I walked to one of the library shelves and pulled down the ninth book from the far end on the second shelf. The book was entitled *Alexander the Great*, by Arthur Weigall. Filed neatly among its three hundred and fifty-three pages were twenty portraits of Ben Franklin, my favorite printer. I counted out ten of them and let the other ten rest amidst the glory that was Greece.

I had no notion of parting with that money, but Sport might insist on taking a hinge at it before he started giving me the low-down on Colin Alderdyce and Fedona — whoever the hell he, or she, was.

I knew that Mason had the morals of a goat, was most likely a murderer and probably was setting some sort of trap for me. Maybe he mistook me for a primitive innocent. Well, I wasn't that, but maybe I was goofy as a three-headed chimpanzee for going out there alone.

I had thought about inviting Lieutenant Myron Garter, but quickly dismissed the thought because there might be something about the Alderdyce family that I wouldn't want Myron or anybody else to know.

I folded the Franklins neatly and put them in the left pocket of my pants. I wanted the right hand to be free in case I needed to draw my hole card.

I pulled out the Elgin, pressed the stem. The lid flipped open just like it always does.

Plenty of time. But I would have done it even if there weren't.

I called my mother.

"Alex," she said, "I was just looking at you, a picture of you in that old photograph album I brought from Akron. You know the one I'm talking about; you were in high school and you just bought your first automobile. I'm looking at it right now. What kind of car was that?"

"Olds '88."

"Uh, huh. What color? I can't tell from this. It's black and white."

"Blue, remember, Mom. Blue and white, the colors of the Greek flag, you used to say."

"Oh yes, I remember now. And that girl standing there next to you. What was her name? You were going to the dance."

"It was the senior prom. Cathy. Cathy Kerr was her name."

"I guess so. You looked handsome, Alex. You still do. I wonder whatever happened to Cathy Kerr."

"She went to Ohio State and married a football player named Radovitch and had a bunch of little Radovitches."

"Speaking of getting married . . ."

"There's somebody I want you to meet, Mom."

"Alex! Is she there now? Put her on the phone, I'll say hello . . . what's her name?"

"No, Mom, she's not here, but I think you'll like her. Her name is Goldie, Goldie Rose, but her real name is Triandafelos . . ."

"Alex, you make my heart beat faster . . ."

"She has the same effect on me . . . you'll meet her soon, but I got to go now to see somebody."

"Goldie?"

"No. Somebody else. An albatross that's been hanging on my back. I love you, Mom. Goodnight."

As I walked out the door I could feel the wings of that albatross beating on my back.

In case I didn't make it through the night, I wanted my mother to know there was a Goldie Rose, just in case they met at my funeral.

Chapter Thirty-Six

Mandeville Canyon is the other side of UCLA and this side of the Pacific Ocean. For me that night, between a rock and a hard place. I just hoped the rock wasn't a tombstone.

I turned onto Fox Hill Lane just a few minutes late, hoping that Mason would already be there. That would give me a chance to reconnoiter adroitly and size up the set-up. But of course he wasn't. He wanted to do the sizing up.

I drove to the fourth light and parked. But I didn't park directly under it as he had instructed. If he was going to throw a shot or shots at me I didn't want to be in a spotlight.

Just out of habit I checked the cylinder of the .38 Special for the third time. It was still loaded. I got out of the LeBaron, closed the door, looked up and down the empty road — and waited.

I felt like a fried oyster waiting to be swallowed. I tried not to keep touching the .38 Special in my belt under the coat. But the feel of it was so damn reassuring. He let me cool my moccasins for a few minutes. I stood there listening to the night noises. Birds and crickets and I don't know what.

Then it came. From out of the black night and from the opposite side of the road. A car coming down the hill, first fast, then slow. Slower. Closer, until it was about fifteen yards from me and the LeBaron. Just close enough for me to make out a figure at the wheel.

From where I was standing I was a sitting duck.

He'd never have a better shot and he took it. Only it wasn't a shot. It was shots. A barrage of bullets from the Uzi braced against the open window.

I dropped and rolled against the bottom side of the LeBaron while gunfire smashed windows and punctured holes across the fuselage of the car. Shards of glass covered me like confetti at a conquering hero's parade. But I didn't feel like any conquering hero. I felt like crawling deep into that cement foxhole. And that's what I tried to do.

The car picked up speed and streaked down the road and I fired at it a couple of times with the .38, but I didn't even come close. The car was too far away and my hand was shaking like a malt mixer, so was the rest of me.

Then it was quiet. All the night sounds had stopped. The birds and the crickets and I don't know what, all seemed to be holding their breath. But not me. I was breathing for all I was worth. I wanted to keep on breathing just to make sure that I was still alive.

I don't know how long I lay there splattered with glass, necking with the cement, but I was in no hurry. I didn't think he'd come back and I sure as hell had no chance of playing hound to his fox. It wasn't him I was going after anyhow, at least not directly.

Okay, Night, I finally said to myself paraphrasing Philip Marlowe, you're a tough guy. You've been slugged in the head, shot in the leg, bounced around by a Bull. You've been lied to and triple-crossed until you're as silly as a pair of waltzing wallflowers. You've been jerked and joggled and shot at again and you don't know whom to trust, but by the grace of the great Jehovah you're still alive. There's just one thing to do. Get up, brush yourself off and start all over again.

And I knew just where to start.

A few minutes later I was driving what was left of my car onto Ambassador Drive. I pulled into the Alderdyce estate and parked in front of the main entrance just like I was part of the family. I walked up to the door, pressed the button and let the chimes ring out.

There was no alternative. I had to confront the only link I had to Mase and the mysterious Mister or Miz Fedona. Even if it meant breaking a promise to a nice old lady who was dying.

I guess I wasn't very nice to dear old Peter when he opened the door. I didn't waste any time with greetings. I just asked if Mrs. Alderdyce or Colin or both of them were home. He was startled by my appearance and attitude and mumbled something that included "library." That's all I wanted to know.

I elbowed my way past Peter and his feeble protest and proceeded along the Camino Real. I opened the library door without bothering to knock. I had neither the time nor the inclination to observe amenities.

Mrs. Alderdyce was sitting in her chair by the fireplace. Colin sat across in the opposite chair. When I broke in Colin rose, drink in hand. I shoved him back into his chair and he spilled some of his drink onto his velvet smoking jacket but I didn't much care.

"Sit down, Colin; I've had it with you!"

"For heaven's sake, Alex!" Mrs. A. exclaimed, but I didn't pay her any attention. I concentrated on Colin.

"Your pal Mason just tried to blow me away — again. It's getting to be a nasty habit . . ."

"Alex!" Mrs. Alderdyce stood up.

"I've got a little speech to make, Mrs. A., no matter who gets hurt, you or me or Colin or somebody else or all of us. It's got to come out in the open and it can't wait. Now I've got a little theory. It goes like this . . ."

"Alex, please, just let me . . ."

"Let him talk, Mother."

"Just try and stop me. Now according to my little theory, Colin here hires Mase and Burke to play fake cops and heist the jewels on New Year's night. But it doesn't happen. A private dick gets in the way and Burke lands in the hospital." I walked toward the fireplace, then turned back. "Mase is afraid his buddy'll spill the beans, so he tosses him off the roof. Maybe the cops'll buy it as suicide, maybe they won't, but he's rid of him. It so happens that Mase is playing house with Burke's wife anyway. I've made her acquaintance, she's a sweet little thing right out of Sunnybrook Farm . . . I need a drink."

"Help yourself," said Colin ever the gracious host. I moved to the bar and found a bottle of bourbon.

"You, Mrs. A., want to find out about the corpse and his family. That's all right with Colin, there's not much he can do about it anyhow — until I also sniff out Mason. Mason doesn't like that. That's when Colin tells you to tell me to lay off. But it's too late because Mason decides to get rid of me tonight up in Mandeville Canyon. He misses and that's what brings me here."

I took a swallow from the glass of bourbon and walked back toward the fireplace. I let the bourbon and my theory settle for a few seconds.

"Of course," I continued, "there are some things I don't know, like where somebody named Fedona fits in." I turned and faced Mrs. Alderdyce. "Mrs. A., I'd do just about anything for you. But your son is a no-good bastard. I don't know how it happened, but it happened. Just like red hair." I took another lungful of bourbon. "Well, what do you think of my little theory?"

"It's very good," said Mrs. Alderdyce and sat back down in her chair. "Except for one thing."

"What's that?"

"I was part of the whole scheme."

I looked at Colin. Maybe he was smiling and maybe he wasn't. Either way he was still a no-good bastard.

"I don't believe it," I said to her. "You're covering up for him," and turned back to Colin. "And you'd let her."

"Alex," Mrs. A. said in a quiet voice, "they never had the jewels."

"Sure they did. I saw you give them to 'em."

"That's what you were supposed to see. In the back seat I slipped them into my purse and put on the fakes."

"What fakes?"

"That's where Fedona comes in," said Colin. "He made up the fakes. He's in the jewelry business, among other things."

"You see, Alex," Mrs. A. continued in a quiet voice, "we were going to collect the two million insurance."

"And Fedona," Colin said, "would sell the real ones for almost as much. We'd split that part."

"I don't believe it," I said, even though I was beginning to. I knew that she was desperate or she wouldn't be trying to sell the house. But I still wanted to believe that she was taking the fall along with Colin so I'd go easy on her son. But she did her best to convince me otherwise.

"The fakes are in the safe. Do you want me to show them to you?"

"It's true, Night." Colin didn't even wait for me to answer her. "Fedona had hired Mason and Burke at Top Guard to make deliveries. This time he hired them to make the heist. Since you've been driving my mother to that party for years we had no choice. It had to be you, otherwise it would look suspicious. The trouble was . . ."

". . . that I didn't roll over and play dead like a nice doggy."

"I guess you could say that."

"How did you know Fedona?"

"The Tennis Club. I knew he had a shady reputation. One thing just led to another. I'm not sure any more whether it was his idea or mine. But he planned it, right down to the last detail."

"Only it didn't come off according to plan."

"You saw to that. After Mason got rid of Burke he wanted more, much more, to get out of the country. He still wants it and he still thinks he's going to get it in just a few minutes."

"What do you mean?"

"He's going to Fedona's. He plans to get fifty thousand dollars — but Fedona's got other plans."

"Where's Fedona?"

"It's too late."

"Where?" I grabbed Colin and yanked him out of his seat. "Where is Fedona?"

"Six-ten Vesper Street."

I let go of him and he fell back into a clumsy sitting position.

"I'm sorry, Alex," Mrs. Alderdyce whispered.

"Never mind that. Call Lieutenant Garter, find him. At the station, at home or anyplace. Don't tell him any of this. Not a thing. Just say I need help and make it convincing." I moved toward the door.

"Alex," she said. "Don't go."

"I'm going."

"I'll convince him."

Chapter Thirty-Seven

Maybe I wanted to get there in time and maybe I didn't. But I knew I had to go. There were two reasons. There was still the chance that I could get Cynthia Alderdyce out of the mess that she was in. I knew that she was in it because of her rotten son and his tennis chum, Fedona. Also there was the slight case of murder, Burke's. And attempted murder, mine.

I wanted a shot at Mr. Mason. Maybe Fedona would take care of that or maybe Mason would smell a double-cross and get him first. All I could do was guess — until I got there.

While I headed toward Vesper the last part of the patchwork was being stitched into the quilt.

Mason's Honda pulled in front of the Fedona Import-Export Building. The Honda had a different set of license plates. Mason drove. Eunice sat beside him. He switched off the engine.

"When I called I told him to leave it unlocked and wait in the office."

"I still think he's gonna try to pull something."

"Let him try. That's why you're going to do exactly what I said. I'll leave the door unlocked. Where's the piece I gave you?"

"In my purse."

"Put it in your hand."

"Mase . . ."

"What?"

"A kiss for luck."

"Sure baby, and in ten minutes we'll be on our way."

Mason got out of the Honda and made his way to the main entrance of the building. The door was unlocked. He went inside and headed for the hallway that led to Fedona's office. The hallway was dimly lit. Mason knew where the light switch was but he wanted the hall to stay dark.

The door to Fedona's office was open a crack and a line of light came through the edges. Mason stopped just in front of the entrance.

"Mike."

"Come in."

Mason walked into the room. Fedona sat behind his desk and the only light came from a lamp on that desk. And just in front of Fedona on the desk there was a large accordion manila folder, tied with a ribbon of string connected to it. From where he stood Mason looked around the room.

"You tryin' to save on electricity?"

"Every nickel counts. I had to kick in on part of that fifty."

"Where's Alderdyce?"

"He couldn't make it. The money's in there." Fedona pointed to the folder. "Check it out."

"I will." Mason moved toward the folder, both his hands in plain sight.

"You know we've been robbed twice."

"So?" Mason started to untie the folder.

"So," Fedona reached for a gun in the open drawer of his desk. "They say the third time's a charm."

As soon as the gun in his hand cleared the desk a shot sounded through the room. The bullet hit Fedona in the chest. He looked at Mason who stood there, both hands on the folder, then he saw her near the doorway, Eunice holding the gun that had fired.

It happened fast, but not fast enough to keep Fedona from pulling the trigger. Eunice fired again but Fedona's shot hit her in the forehead, dead center. She dropped the gun and fell to the floor. Fedona was already slumped across his desk. Eunice's second shot had finished him.

Mason didn't even bother looking at Eunice. He knew she was a corpse when half her brain sprayed out of the back of her head from the dum-dum. He untied the folder and reached in.

Stacks of newspaper cut to money size.

That's when he heard the sound of running footsteps coming down the hallway. Mine.

I had pulled up outside just in time to listen to the gunfire. Earlier I had reloaded the .38 and it was already in my hand when I ran into the building.

Halfway down the dark hallway I saw Mason coming out of the office. There must not have been another exit. Mason saw me too. We both shot. We both missed. But his didn't miss by far. I ducked into a doorway.

Mason spotted a door marked "STAIRS." He ran for it and headed the only way they went. Up.

I followed into the doorway gun first. The stairway was even darker than the hall. But neither one of us wanted any more light. If we could see we could be seen.

From the landing he fired and I shot into the muzzle of his gun but both our bullets ricocheted around the hall and the iron stairway and rails.

There was a slit of a window on the landing that let a little moonlight streak through, and I saw his crooked shadow cut across the light and race up toward the second story. His footsteps clattered on the metal steps. Mine not as much, I went up slower.

He fired blind again and, two at a time, took the stairs that zigzagged against the narrow walls to the third floor. But this time his blind shot came even closer and I stumbled, almost fell and my bad leg bent with a bolt of pain against the grain. I kept climbing.

Mason made it to the third floor landing and that's all there was except for a heavy iron door with a lock device marked "ATLAS LOCK CO." The lock device had a lever with a flat edge. On the edge two words:

EMERGENCY
STRIKE

I heard Mason slam it with the butt of his gun, then he twisted the doorknob with one hand as he shot back at me crouched against the rail.

When the door opened I had a pretty good view of him framed against the moonlight for about a second and I fired and sparks sprayed off the metal door just behind him. He was on the roof.

As I came through the door Mason shot and ran across the roof, but it was flat and clear and there was no place to hide. I still had the door and I used it for cover, fired twice and heard the bugle call of the seventh cavalry, only it was police sirens. Mason couldn't help hearing them too. To him they must have sounded like "Taps."

He ran to the ledge to see if he could make a jump to another building. But there wasn't any other building.

He was a fish in a barrel. I shot him in the leg. I suppose I could have hollered "Freeze" or "Drop it" or any of that shit but I didn't. I was hoping he'd shoot back and when he did I aimed to the left of his breastbone and squeezed.

He buckled. He swayed like a drunken monkey in the moonlight and fell off the roof.

A couple of seconds later I heard him hit. His gun bounced. He didn't.

I walked to the edge of the roof and looked down. I saw Lieutenant Myron Garter and two uniformed policemen from a black and white parked near Myron's car.

The two officers were looking down at the remains. My friend Myron was looking up at me.

I don't know how I looked, but I felt pretty good. Even the pain in my leg felt pretty good.

Chapter Thirty-Eight

But that's not quite the end of the story that I started to write down. Sometimes it's hard to tell when or where a story ends. It's not like a book or a movie where "The End" is written on a page or screen. Where you close the cover or the picture fades out. Life is different than that.

The inflated white swan floated gracefully in the Alderdyce swimming pool. I walked across the decking toward Lieutenant Myron Garter. There were a couple of police officers, a Medical Examiner from the Coroner's Office and a photographer.

Colin Alderdyce sat at a chair with his head burrowed into his arms at a table. Peter stood beside him.

Two assistants were wheeling away a gurney containing a body covered with a blanket and strapped onto the death carriage.

I stopped near a slipper with a broken heel that was at the edge of the deep side of the pool. Myron left the others and came close.

"I called you as soon as we got the report, Alex."

I just nodded.

"It was the maid's day off," he said. "Her son was at the Tennis Club. She sent Peter to the store. So she was alone. Walked by the pool, her heel broke. She stumbled, fell into the deep end. She couldn't swim. Must've panicked."

I didn't say anything.

"Well," Garter shrugged, "that's the way it looks."

"Yeah," I said. "That's the way it looks."

"I know how much you liked her, Alex, but these things happen."

"Yeah."

"She lived a good life."

"Every minute — almost."

"What?"

"Nothing. Thanks, Myron."

I turned and walked away. I didn't go through the house. I didn't want to. When I got around the corner I stopped and took a piece of folded paper out of my pocket. She had sent it by messenger that morning. By the time it arrived she knew it would be too late for me to stop her.

I unfolded the letter and read it again:

Dear Alex,

You are right. He is a bastard but as the old saying goes, "he's my bastard."

I'm going for a good stretch of the legs with my wildcatter.

Love,
Cynthia

I folded the letter and put it back into my pocket. I walked toward the LeBaron parked in the driveway.

It took a lot of courage, but she had it. Instead of death by natural causes — this way Colin would collect twice as much from the insurance policy. For her "accidental" death he'd collect double indemnity.

I got into the LeBaron and started to drive away from the Alderdyce mansion that now belonged to Colin.

Afraid of the water as she was, she jumped in and made the final sacrifice for her son — a lot of courage. She was a spicy old tomato.

As I turned onto Ambassador Drive I thought of her, and the floating white swan.

A few days later a messenger from Tri Arc came to the office and handed me an envelope. There was a note inside.

Stuff from Carmel looks great. Frances is sensational.

We both owe you.

Mike

Also there was a check for five thousand dollars. One door closes, another door opens.

I made reservations and took Briny Marlin to dinner at La Fiore in Beverly Hills. Jean Leon, the owner and an old friend of mine, was leading us to our table. But something happened.

I saw Colin Alderdyce with a beautiful lady, not Miss Sweden, sitting at a booth. I stopped, long enough to make sure that Colin noticed me. He hesitated as long as he could but finally had to look up.

"Hello, Alex . . . this . . . this is . . . I'd like . . ."

I grabbed him, pulled him up from his chair, slugged him and knocked him halfway under another table, spilling food and drinks. As he looked up at me blood leaked out of his mouth and onto his shirt and tie.

"Have a good time, Colin," I said. "Your mother picked up the check." I took Goldie by the hand and started for the door. "Cancel our reservations, Jean. And send me a bill for the damage."

We picked up a couple of submarines and some beer and I took Goldie up to the office. I told her there was something there that I had written, and I wanted her to read it.

We ate the sandwiches and drank the beer and she read the whole story just as I remembered it and wrote it. From Palm Desert to the swan floating in the pool. Even the part about Frances Vale.

While she read I thought about what Nick Charles said when Nora wondered what became of people left over after murders. He answered that they go on being pretty much the people they were before. Murder doesn't round out anybody's life except the murdered's and sometimes the murderer's.

I thought to myself, Colin will still go on being Colin, but thanks to his mother he can afford it, at least for a while. My mother will still go on being my mother. It looked like Myron and Rhoda were going to try it again. They were even going to a fat farm together. E. Elliott Elliot will go on with his walking stick and epigrams. Morgan Noble will go on "borrowing" his trade papers. Wes Weston will go on waiting for westerns, and the Bernstein twins will go on finishing each other's sentences. Mrs. Kramer will go on mixing her tobacco and telling me to quit smoking cigarettes. Frances Vale will go on acting — maybe win an Academy Award. I didn't know how many of my old clients would keep looking me up. I hadn't heard from Tawny Tucker — yet. And I wasn't sure what would happen to Briny Marlin and me.

When she finished reading what I had written, she came over and kissed me.

"Keep writing," she said. "You're good, kid. You're very good."

"You know that nobody'll ever read it but you."

"The important thing is that you wrote it."

"Yeah, I did."

"Keep writing, and if you ever need anything, just whistle. You know where I'll be, don't you?"

"Right across the hall?"

"Closer than that, Alex. Much closer."

"Hey, that's what Edward G. Robinson said to Fred MacMurray at the end in *Double Indemnity*."

"So he did. Now I'll tell you something he didn't say."

"What?"

"Take me home, Alex, and we'll look at the rainbow."

"What rainbow? It hasn't rained in months."

"Maybe you were misinformed."

"Maybe I was."

She was right. We went to her place and spent the night on a rainbow.

The next morning I was back in the office. I went to the window and looked out at Rodeo Drive and the other streets. There was the beige Bentley and E. Elliott Elliot and all the other people of Beverly Hills. All right, friends and neighbors, natives and pilgrims, I'm here and I'm going to stay here, at least for a while. I'm going to do a little writing.

Then I went to the typewriter and sat down. So what if I could never show anybody the one story that I had written? It was only one story. There are a million stories with their tongues hanging out, waiting to be written.

I started to write . . .

The telephone rang.

About the Author

Andrew J. Fenady, fresh out of college in the 1950s, went to work in Los Angeles for journalist–TV personality Paul Coates as a leg man/trouble shooter, and all 'round factotum in the creation and production of *Confidential File*, a local, then national expose television series that was the precursor to *60 Minutes* and other investigative programs. Fenady wrote and produced more than 150 episodes, which won 3 Emmys. The documentaries directed by Irvin Kershner took the two of them from the kid gangs of Watts and the alleys of South Central to the sophistry of the Sunset Strip and the night lights of Beverly Hills — and led to Fenady writing and producing his first feature, the acclaimed *Stakeout on Dope Street*.

Then for a couple of decades Fenady went Western, creating, writing and producing several TV series, among them: *The Rebel*, *Branded*, *Hondo*, as well as western features including *Chisum* for John Wayne.

Fenady returned to the mean streets with

his novel and feature film *The Man With Bogart's Face*, which won the Mystery Writers of America Edgar Award.

Now, after a dozen highly successful western novels, Fenady mixes the movie stars he's known and worked with — Robert Mitchum, Charles Bronson, Angie Dickinson, Angela Lansbury and many others — with *roman à clef* characters in a knuckle busting novel ranging from Palm Springs to skid row to Beverly Hills.